ZONE ROUGE

A BONE-CHILLING COLLECTION OF
18 SHORT HORROR STORIES

ALPHONSE SCHALLER

Hylosis Publishing LLC
hylosis.pub

ISBN eBook: 979-8-89403-012-8

ISBN Paperback: 979-8-89403-013-5

ISBN Hardcover: 979-8-89403-014-2

This is a work of fiction. Names, characters, places, and incidents portrayed are the product of the author's imagination or are used fictitiously. Any resemblance to actual persons (living or deceased), establishments, events, products, or locales is entirely coincidental and unintended.

No generative AI was used in the creation of this book's content.

TABLE OF CONTENTS

ZONE ROUGE

01

UNCANNY VALLEY

There are two basic types of predation: pursuit and ambush. The first is what most people, I think, picture when a predator comes to mind. A cheetah running down a zebra, a wolf pack nipping at the sides of a moose. Even insects such as the dragonfly hunt mosquitoes and other smaller dragonflies.

Humans were pursuit predators once, though it's more commonly referred to as *persistence hunting*. We followed beasts over miles of terrain—the sweat on our skins releasing heat more efficiently than the panting tongues of our prey—and eventually killed the animal and brought it back to our tribes.

The second type of predator is an ambush predator. A crocodile, lurking in the river for a wildebeest, or a trapdoor spider waiting for an insect to land on its door. These are camouflage predators, the water of the river concealing the scaly back of the reptile, the spider dragging grass over the web. But what's interested me for the past weeks, ever since I went hiking, are predators that use a different method.

Aggressive mimicry. An evolution where predatory animals have developed the ability to send signals to their prey in a method that the prey will dismiss as harmless or friendly, allowing the predator to close in and feed upon the unfortunate animal. Anglerfish are the most famous example, the bioluminescent light dangling from the top of its head having become shorthand for danger, for a lure pulling in a victim. But they're not the only ones. The snapping turtle's tongue looks like a worm, and so fish swim eagerly into its mouth. The vibrant colors of the inside of the Venus flytraps mouth make it look like a flower to the insects it preys on. The point is: for predators like this, they have to signal to their prey that they're harmless. Friendly. *Not to be feared.*

I was hiking in the mountains of northeast Vermont, near the Canadian border. It's a lovely place, especially in the last days of summer, though perhaps hotter than I'd like. For all that I was a New England boy, born and raised, the summers and springs were always my least favorite part. I'd driven up by myself, begging off a scheduled trip to Burlington that some college friends invited me to. We all went to university in the state and had decided to come back a week early to spend some time together. It was the last day, and while I wouldn't say any of my other friends were uninterested in the great outdoors, they were all more interested in thrifting along college town streets than hiking the interweaving mountain trails until the sun started to set.

There had been no other cars in the parking lot of the trailhead, the dust settling as I pulled in and locked my car before looking about. The sun had just finished completely rising over the horizon, and I slipped on a baseball cap and applied sunscreen, grimacing as the white spray bottle began to sputter. Back in my backpack it went, alongside pocketknife, flashlight, and compass, and I stepped onto the trails.

I was alone on the trails for seven hours. I followed the creek as far as I could, spotting multiple deer and even a fox or two sneaking through the undergrowth. The dappled sunlight that shone through the canopy was much appreciated, shielding me from the burning sun, and I made a bit of a game out of seeing how far I could get without having to cross an expanse of shadeless grass. There's a certain pleasure about exploring a small section of wilderness without having to actually get lost and endanger yourself.

Squirrels chittered and ran back and forth along the branches of the trees, and one genuinely startled me when it ripped of a chunk of bark the size of my palm. It fell on my head, and I yelped, starting in just the right way to send me tripping to the ground, knees and hands hitting the ground with a heavy thud. Hissing from the pain, I glanced at my hands. Only some minor scrapes meant that it could be safely ignored, and with a grunt, I hurled the bark back up into the trees, causing the squirrels to take off, shaking the leaves from the branches.

Grumbling, I decided this was a good a place as any for a lunch, and sat on a nearby log, sighing with exasperation when I saw the grass stains on my pants. Brushing it off as best I could, I slung off my backpack and opened it up. I had brought some salami, some cheese, crackers and trail mix—a standard hiking lunch in my family.

From the side pocket, I grabbed my pocketknife. I had a Swiss Army in my actual pocket, but this was a four-inch folding knife, one that I kept in my backpack *just in case*. The handle was orange plastic, with finger grips curved into the material, and the click that sounded out as the mechanism activated to keep the blade firm sounded loud in the natural soundscape. I remember it clearly. Unsurprising, perhaps, but still weird.

I had been sitting there, snacking on cracker sandwiches for what couldn't have been more than four minutes, when for the first time all day, I heard footsteps. There's an unmistakable sound when a hiking boot crunches leaves, the plastic nubs and grooves forming a pattern unlike anything in nature, and there's really no way to mistake it for anything else. Turning, I made to greet the person coming up on the trail behind me and stopped, the words failing to come out of my mouth.

There was something off about the man standing on the trail, something that triggered that lizard part of my brain wanting to run, to fight, to freeze—to abandon the sapience of humanity and bound away into the trees. The first thing I noticed was his shirt: it was inside out and back to front, the tag fluttering in the soft breeze as we stared at each other. It was too large for him by far, the hem hanging down past his waist and nearly to the tips of his fingers. Ripped jeans, stained with mud and grass, seemed to be equally big, and I could only assume the grace of a belt stopped them from tangling his ankles. Those boots were untied, but the laces looked like they were tucked into the boots themselves to prevent him from tripping.

He might have been shorter than me by a head, but I didn't like the way he was staring at me. It reminded me too much of the way the people on the subway would stare at me, the ones who mumbled to themselves and were clearly not mentally well. Brown hair hung from his scalp, tangled and twisted and visibly unwashed. I swear, I couldn't tell when he blinked.

"Can I help you?" I asked, hand tightening around my knife. This was not my normal reaction, but this man was anything but normal. I would have offered him some crackers, asked him how the trails were treating him, where he had come from… but there was a part of me screaming that something was wrong, that this man wasn't right. It was a combination of his clothes and the way he moved. Ultimately, I can try to justify it all I like. The truth is, I didn't trust him. I thought he was dangerous. And I was right.

"Hello," he said, taking a step toward me.

I blinked. His voice was slightly throaty, the word mildly accented. But it was still a word, a greeting, something that my subconscious recognized as a symbol of harmlessness. And my hand loosened my grip on my knife.

That was when he moved, sprinting at me at breakneck speed, boots slamming against the ground and arms pumping back and forth. Yelping, I stumbled backward, holding out the knife in front of me like a spear. A spear the man slammed into with seemingly no regard for his own safety. The shining tip of the blade pressing into his chest, piercing through fabric, then through skin—continuing forward, as if there was no ribcage under his skin. It was like he was a boar running directly into a spear, unable to even understand what he was looking at, even as he slammed into me, barreling me over as a squeal came from his mouth.

My back was pressed against the ground, all air forced from my lungs with the force of a cannon, and in that moment, I thought that I would never be able to inhale again. That thing's face was inches above mine, and was so deep into the uncanny valley it must have been at the very bottom of the thing. I can barely describe what was wrong with it. Just a complete and utter sense of the proportions of the face being off: the left eye being ever so slightly higher than the right, the nose somehow off-center, the mouth too wide to be that of a human. Those eyes were light green and looked like my brother's. More than anything else, that might be what makes me shiver the most when I think back on it now, just how human those eyes were with how inhuman it was.

Its mouth was open in a frozen squeal in that moment, so much saliva dropping from the lips of the things that it looked like the spit-up of a baby. Its teeth: sharp and needle pointed, resembling that of a lamprey or a moray. A single, bizarre thought popped into my head, and I wondered if this thing was a vampire, with those blood-draining teeth. It had a tongue, but not a human-like one, broad and flat. It was more like that of a snake, completely straight but for the forked tip.

The shirt was loose and baggy and torn with a bloodstain. The image of this thing wearing my shirt inside out, stained with my blood, flashed through my mind, and despite there being no more air in my lungs I tried my best to scream as loud as I possibly could. That's the frozen moment I remember, like a snapshot of what could have been the last second I was ever alive. But thankfully, my knife was in my hands, and steel won the day over that creature.

The sound that came from its mouth when my blade plunged into its chest was unholy, exactly what I'd imagine came from a slaughterhouse day in and day out, and the thing jumped back, my knife still lodged in its chest. My kick came a second too late, my leg striking out at thin air as the thing got far enough away to avoid the sole of my hiking boot. Pawing at it, the creature stumbled, managing to close its fingers around the handle and pull it out—but not straight out. Downward, ripping through even more of its flesh in the process and eliciting an even louder cry.

I've been cut deep before. An accident with a kitchen knife when I worked as a line cook, one that resulted in stitches across the meat of my forearm. I've seen what it should look like when flesh parts from flesh, when blood spills from severed veins and capillaries. It didn't look like what was under that thing's skin. It looked more like raw chicken—pink and clean. It huffed in pain, shaking as it dropped to its knees and pressed its hands against its wound in a manner that was far too human. Scrambling to my feet, I backed away, and for a strange, insane moment, thought about running to retrieve my knife. Now, though, there was no force on earth that could compel me to get closer to that inhuman thing on the floor, and so I fled, leaving its bleating behind.

I can barely remember my flight from the forest, only the frantic sound of my boots hitting the dirt trail, the desperate flickering of my vision as I pushed myself as far as I could go, following the signs leading back to the trailhead without a single thought for cutting through the forest. There was no chance I was leaving the safety of the trails.

Staggering into the parking lot, my car was still the only one there. I rushed to it, finally letting my feet stop moving as I leaned against it, panting for breath. My lungs were aching, my legs burning from heel to thigh, a stitch like fire burning under my chest. But I was away from that thing, and I held onto that thought as I unlocked the car and spilled into it, driving away as fast as I could.

I haven't told anyone this. How could I? It's utterly insane, and if anything, the person I told would just say I came across some psycho in the woods, and my fight or flight kicked in, making them look inhuman in the heat of stress. It's well known, after all, how fallible memory truly is, how the mind twists itself to form a narrative. I have no physical proof, no photo of those inhuman teeth, no audio of that bestial screaming. And even if I did, who would believe me with how well video and sound effects can be manipulated today? Even high schoolers were making names for themselves on the internet with their skills. But I know what happened.

Aggressive mimicry. It's the practice of predatory animals attempting to signal to their prey in their own manner of communication that they aren't a threat. That there's nothing wrong, no jaws waiting to snap shut, no claws ready to swing down. I've thought about it a lot in the days since that encounter I had on the trails, done research on other creatures that perform it, to the point that I'm lagging behind on my actual classes.

But that's what that thing was. Something that preys on humans with no idea what the word "hello" means beyond a series of sounds that will make its prey less likely to run. It evolved to mimic aspects of human behavior, copying greetings and body language, each generation refining it as the ones that couldn't properly adapt failed to find food and pass on their genes. Even as humanity itself refined its ability to detect them. That phenomenon we call the uncanny valley: a prickling sensation in the back of our minds telling us that what we're looking at is a predator specifically designed to hunt us.

There's one thing, though, that I can't seem to figure out. It was wearing clothing. Probably the clothing of previous victims, sure. But still. It wore clothes. And if others of that species figure out that they can put on clothing… if they evolve faster than we can convince each other that they exist…

I think I'm going to keep an eye on how many people go missing while hiking. Just in case.

02

THE COUNCILORS

Theatre folk tend to be quite the superstitious bunch. It doesn't matter if they're an actor, a director, or one of the many types of techs or backstage workers, we are one and all slaves to lady luck. There are those rituals that everyone has heard of, even as a mild curiosity: the referring to *Macbeth* as "the Scottish play," wishing for your compatriots to "break a leg" instead of wishing them "good luck," never whistling inside the theatre.

Then there are those tidbits of information that one doesn't learn in high-school theatre, but elsewhere: the rule about never allowing a peacock feather on stage, leaving a single light on even as the theatre is closed, and banning the use of blue costumes. Then there are the most obscure ones, the ones that vary from theatre to theatre, with every production having its own rules. And finally, there is the story of *The Councilors.*

The Councilors is the most common name, but I've also heard it called by half a dozen other ones besides. When I worked briefly in New York City, they knew it as *Heir to Naught*, while in Los Angeles they called it *Heavy is the Crown*. No matter what, though, the plot is roughly the same.

The Councilors is set in ancient Greece, meaning the play could have been written from any time from Sophocles to Shakespeare, and the city-state remains unnamed throughout. It opens with the chorus informing us that the king waged war upon his neighbors three times, once every seven years, and at the end of the last battle he vanished. Though he has a wife, he has only daughters, and now his councilors begin to fight for position, all seeking to marry the king's eldest daughter, Arsinoe, and succeed him.

There are four primary councilors. The first is Lysimachus, a general of the king who went with him on each of his campaigns, and whom the other councilors suspect of murdering the king in the confusion of battle. The second is Polykarpos, a landowner and farmer who feeds much of the city with his grain, and who is making veiled threats to begin selling his grain to rival cities if he loses. The third is Basileios, a nobleman who is on good terms with the city's nobility and has them in his pocket, meaning that the general support of the upper class for him to be king is strong. The fourth and final is Nikolaos, the youngest member of the council given the seat after he saved the king's life in the second campaign. Nikolaos had the closest relationship with the king of the four councilors, in addition to the support of the common folk.

The majority of the play deals with these four scheming with and against each other, and it seems like everyone has heard at least one scheme that someone else hasn't. I, for instance, was shocked when an ex-girlfriend of mine asked me if I remembered the scene where Basileios convinces the nobility to masturbate onto the fields of Polykarpos, thus making the claim that the next harvest belongs to them as the ones who impregnated the earth with the bounty of grain. I myself had the pleasure of telling my stage manager in Los Angeles all about the scene where Lysimachus and Nikolaos wrestle for the amusement and support of the king's second daughter, Korinna, making fools of themselves before she leaves without backing either.

These schemes, however, are ribbons around the maypole of the main plot. At the end of the first act, a young man comes to the city-state, claiming to bear the king's sword, shield, crown, and armor. Each is confirmed as legitimate, and the councilors flatter him heavily, seeking to praise the young man so as to impress the king's widow, Metrodora. However, at the end of the audience, the young man introduces himself as Theokritos, and reveals the king's first crown, thought lost during the first campaign twenty-one years ago, which he says proves him to be the king's son, sired on the princess of that conquered city.

Immediately, the councilors turn on him, and order his execution for lies and forgery, which Theokritos does not protest, simply noting that the hypocrisy of the councilors is now laid bare in a monologue. His head is struck from his body, and each of the four councilors lay claim to one of the items he brought with him—Lysimachus the sword, Polykarpos the shield, Basileios the crown, and Nikolaos the armor, while the lost crown is discarded as a forgery and picked up by the king's third daughter, Sophia.

The tone of the play is hard to understand. It starts as a comedy, certainly, a satire of democracy and the scheming, conniving councilors willing to do just about anything to step into the position of power left vacant without a clear successor. The schemes in the first act certainly are farcical enough. A third scheme I know of is one in which Nikolaos attempts to convince Metrodora that the king had told him he was to marry Arsinoe when they returned from campaign, and Polykarpos claims the same, though neither knows anything personal at all about the young woman. The councilors frequently assert one thing, and then when contradicted by the queen or the princesses, fall over themselves to insist that they didn't say what just came out of their mouths—not at all. In fact, they were testing the other councilors, and the fact that they weren't corrected is proof of their failure. It is a genuinely funny play, at the beginning. That does change, though.

In the second act, Theokritos appears as a vision to Metrodora, Arsinoe, Korinna, and Sophia, reiterating his claim of being the king's son. He informs them that the gods are displeased with the squabbling of the councilors, and if the rightful king is not on the throne by the end of the year, the city will be destroyed.

The four councilors are skeptical of this claimed vision, but that night, each is visited by Theokritos, who tells each of them individually they are the rightful king. Lysimachus by his victories on the battlefield, Polykarpos by his feeding of the city, Basileios by his ties with the nobility, and Nikolaos by the former king's trust in him. He cautions each of them not to speak of his appearance to any other, and each councilor gives a soliloquy to the audience about their confidence in their claim.

It is at this point, theatre folk whisper to each other, that the play gets strange. The schemes that were farcical in the first act become vicious and cruel in the second. And yet, no one can agree on what schemes were in the text… because each is different. The legend is that starting with the second act of the play, the motivations and backstories of each of the councilors, princesses, and the widowed queen come up, and each is similar to that of the actor or actress playing the character. And it makes sense, for theatre communities tend to be incestuous by nature; we date in our circle, we break up in our circle, we fight and make up together… and so there are plenty of dramas for *The Councilors* to latch onto.

Once, it's said, the man playing Polykarpos had cheated on his girlfriend—another actress, of course, though accounts vary as to whether or not she was in the play. It was with someone who worked backstage, and so when it came time for the play to be performed in that theatre, Nikolaos swept in during the second act and accused Polykarpos of being unfaithful to his late wife. In the end, Polykarpos admitted to his infidelity and bragged about it. "If I take a hundred mistresses and sire a hundred children, I shall still be king, for it is he who controls the bounty of the earth that rules over its people!"

I've heard of a version where Metrodora is stopped from taking her own life by the councilors, not because they are concerned for her but because without her as a guiding influence, the race to become king will be far more violent and destructive. She begs to be allowed to go to her husband in death, but they refuse and post a guard with her at all times to ensure she cannot commit suicide. The actress supposedly tried to kill herself as well.

In another story, Lysimachus is accused of knowingly sending soldiers under him to their deaths, so that they would perish, and he would receive the glory that by all rights should have gone to them. Basileios bands the nobles of the city together, and one by one, Lysimachus is forced to give their families the honors of their dead sons that he had taken, and by the end swore bloody vengeance on Basileios and his companions. The actor playing Lysimachus, they say, had lied about his credits, and bribed a thug to attack another actor who he was serving as an understudy for in order to get on stage. The type of thing that happens in dramas about actors, not in real life.

But that's the joke about *The Councilors*; it's a reflection of the theatre company you're in, a reflection of the production. Well, I say joke. But it's not a joke, not at all. Not to me, not anymore. I think that's the good thing about being generally disliked. You're not attached to that web of complex relationships, you can stand to the side as they all tangle up together, making a rope to hang themselves with.

I had just signed on with the theatre company when they decided to run *The Councilors*. I auditioned for the part of Sophia: the third and final daughter of the king. Quiet, thoughtful, and wise. The only one who understands—as early as when Theokritos gets his head chopped off—that there cannot possibly be a happy ending for the city and who gets crushed under the burden, until eventually she throws herself into the sea and drowns herself—though the incident that causes her to do so changes from play to play.

I got the part and received the enmity of the majority of the cast and crew as well. Maggie Brennan had wanted the part since the company had announced it on the schedule. Everyone liked Maggie more than they cared about getting to know the new girl who had just arrived. I don't blame them, and I certainly never wanted anything like this to happen. I would have felt the same, in their shoes. And apparently, just a mild distaste for someone isn't a strong enough emotion to… what, trigger the curse? That's the only thing I can think of as to why I survived. Why when I leaped from the parapet, instead of landing in the cushions prepared for me, I landed in water so cold my heart almost stopped. And yet, somehow survived to cough frantically, shivering until in the aftermath I was found.

But I'm getting ahead of myself here. Act two ends with the death of the widowed queen, sometimes poisoned, sometimes stabbed, always murdered, with suspicion falling immediately upon the four councilors. Each of them had the motive to kill the queen, each of them had the means to do so, and rumblings are beginning to stir both the general citizenry and nobility alike, who are growing tired of even their champions Basileios and Nikolaos.

The third act opens the chorus telling the audience that public rioting has begun. After so many schemes, the citizenry now no longer believes that the councilors that they supported have their interests at heart and desire the return of the old king.

Their representative, an old man named Irenaeus, declares that Theokritos has appeared to him in a vision, and urged him to restore order to the city. It is no longer safe for the councilors to be seen in public, and their schemes ramp up in savagery and viciousness once more. Death comes in earnest, now, and many secondary characters die as the councilors plot the deaths of the others' allies.

In one version I've heard, Nikolaos and Lysimachus join forces for a moment to slaughter many of Basileios's supporters, before returning to find their families poisoned and dying, courtesy of Polykarpos, who also finds his favorite servant has been bribed by Basileios to betray him. The schemes are no longer amusing, not in the slightest, and the mask of civility that the councilors wore has dropped, revealing only the slavering jaws and deep snarls of a wild animal desperate to feed.

Across the third act, the princesses of the city perish one by one. Sophia jumps into the sea, drowning herself, as I said before. In the version we performed, she threw herself from the balcony because of her knowledge that with the passing of her mother and father, there are no longer any who care for her. Arsinoe's husband, whomever it might be, will be king of the city, and have the right to marry her off to whomever he chooses, selling her like a common slave in the marketplace. She is only valued for her position as princess, now, and none who love her have the power to change that. She then throws herself into the ocean, drowning herself and perishing.

Korinna is stabbed to death, usually by a jilted lover or stalker. Our version took the jilted lover line, wherein the princess is found in bed with a soldier, who is executed for the crime of rape, despite Korinna's protests of her consent. The willful princess gets confronted by Nikolaos, and though he professes his love for her, she rejects him entirely. In his rage, the councilor stabs her to death and absconds with her corpse, to the utter despair of her older sister.

Arsinoe, despite the councilors locking her in her chambers, manages to escape onto the streets of the city, where she speaks once more with Theokritos. In some versions, she curses him for coming to the city and instigating the escalation of the scheming and plotting of the councilors, while in another, she offers apologies for her inability to save his life. The latter was the version we went with, and I'm truly not ashamed to admit that the actress who played Arsinoe, Taylor, did such an excellent job I let out tears during rehearsal. Upon conclusion of this con-versation, she slits her own throat in the public square, and the city erupts in a general riot that overwhelms even the councilors, hiding away in their homes.

The mob captures the councilors and brings them to the city square where Arsinoe's corpse still lies. Theokritos appears, visible by all, and launches into a monologue in which he castigates each of the councilors for their crimes. At first—as the story goes—he speaks to each of the councilors about the crimes they committed prior to the opening of the play. Lysimachus, he accuses of pushing the king to wage war in hopes of the king dying in battle, thus causing suffering to thousands in service of his own honor. Polykarpos, he indicts on charges of selling grain at an impossible price for many families to meet, resulting in the starvation of dozens of citizens as a result of his greed. Basileios, he charges with covering up the crimes of nobility to earn their favor, making dozens of people suffer at the hands of noble depravity. Nikolaos, he prosecutes with multiple rapes, murders, and tortures, using his status as the king's confidant to escape suspicion.

Then Theokritos continues, speaking to the schemes that the councilors have participated in and perpetrated throughout the play. Then, the story goes, he begins to speak on the lives of the actors. How they have lied, cheated, and abused those around them. How they have ruined lives, scarred innocents, and traumatized those who they've come into contact with. Every slight is magnified into a true offense, every minor instance of thoughtlessness turned into proof of psychopathy, and every true wrongdoing is amplified into a monument to true evil upon the world. The mob, then, is worked into a frenzy and rushes the councilors, tearing them to pieces with their bare hands. The mob, of course, being the audience.

That's the story. It's a joke, an urban legend. One of those things where a friend of a friend had a friend who played Sophia and was found drowned on dry land. A ghost story, something we tell each other while sleeping overnight at the theatre. That's what I thought.

I think I'm the only one still alive who played a character. I remember… I remember seeing Kayla, who played Queen Metrodora, flee on stage, before being surrounded by those dark silhouettes, and being stabbed, over and over again, her scarlet blood flowing down her dress and onto the wooden stage—and I thought nothing of it. I thought it was normal, and I just watched as someone I cared for died. Taylor, who played Arsinoe… God, her speech was so beautiful, and when she slit her throat with the dagger, there was barely any blood at all, just a single crimson droplet my heart ached to see.

Beth was playing Korinna, and was beaten to death by Nikolaos, his bare hands descending like hammers on her frame, the woman taking the blows in silence until she crumpled, never to move again.

And the four who played the councilors? They were brought up by Theokritos, each one indicted and accused of countless things, and then the audience rose from their seats and ripped them to shreds.

I don't know why I'm still alive. But I think, for now, I'm done with the stage. There is power, after all, in ritual. And what is ritual but a play in which all perform their parts?

03

DAVID

I was first contacted to examine "David" on October 12th, 1990. I believe I received the phone call around ten in the morning, right around the time I was getting ready to leave campus. The course I was teaching that day was a history course on Pompeii, though you can of course look at the records to verify. Not that it particularly matters, except in that I was quite irritated and ready to go home. I no longer wanted to deal with any manner of students or administration matters.

When the phone on the classroom wall rang, I was a fair bit upset—and admittedly, perhaps a bit brusque in my tone when I answered the phone and gave my name.

What I heard, though, was not one of the many secretaries in the office, but Marcus, an old college friend of mine. "Alex!" he nearly shouted, and I remember the tone in his voice. It was the same tone he had used in those wild college days we shared, when he was frightened and excited at the same time. "You have to come out and see me, today! Yesterday, if possible!"

"I have classes," I protested, furrowing my brows.

"You haven't used any of your vacation time, as I know damn well," Marcus countered, and I failed to answer. He was right, of course. I have neither wife nor children, nor other family I care to speak of. I went and did field research during the months in which I had no students due to the various breaks and vacations of colleges, but I hadn't used any of my legally entitled time off in years. "Use some of it and come out to see me. I'm in Arizona, near the border. Fly into Tucson. I'll be there to pick you up. It's important, damn important!"

"Wait!" I hissed, trying to restrain my temper as I could nearly feel the man about to hang up on the other side of the call. "That's not enough. I need more information!"

Marcus sighed. "There's a big find," he told me, "and I want to get our names on it first! Come on, even if it ends up a bust, we haven't seen each other in years. Fly down to Tucson, let me know when your flight is landing, and I'll be there to pick you up!" And after repeating himself, he hung up, leaving me standing there in the empty classroom, staring at the phone until the next professor came in to set up for their own class. I left, nearly forgetting my bags.

Marcus and I went to college together. I was studying anthropology, eventually transitioning to archaeology, and he was studying geology. Two subjects that didn't have much to do with each other to be sure, but we got on well enough. By which I meant that if it were up to me, I would have left my dorm room only for classes, and he was able to pull me out and make me enjoy my time at college. Most importantly, he had what was in my experience the exceptionally rare skill of knowing when to stop pushing and leave me be when I truly was not in the mood for parties or drinking on the quad. So, the fact that Marcus was being exceptionally pushy now, of all times… Well, I have the self-awareness to know I'm not the most socially adept of men, but I did believe something was urgent—or at least, Marcus believed something was urgent.

After a brief stop at the registrar's office and a quick email to my students to notify them of my leave, I headed to the airport. I let Marcus know I would be taking a red-eye and arriving in the early morning, and I did my best to sleep on the flight. I couldn't, though. More likely than not, whatever Marcus thought was a big find would wind up being nothing. But still, frankly speaking, archaeology and anthropology are like gambling. More likely than not, whatever you think is a big find has already been found at another site some years back, or there's simply not enough evidence to classify whatever was found as anything specific and it goes in a pile of artifacts labeled "for ritual purposes." But there's always that one chance you find something with such overwhelming evidence that you completely overturn the conception of a culture or definitively prove something that was only speculated about for years.

And yes, I'll happily admit: there was financial motivation behind it as well. The fields of archaeology and anthropology are the stomping grounds of old men given tenure and job security until they die at 90 years old, spouting their pet theories that barely fit the new evidence. Well, I had gone out on numerous digs, sucked up to numerous professors and doctors who had gotten their Ph.D.s decades ago, and for my labor, I'd gotten a position as a TA at a third-rate college under a second-rate professor. I won't say which one either was—you can look it up— but suffice it to say I was not happy with my choice of career at the time. I deserved better for all the hard work I'd put in, and if that meant I was going to come to Arizona to look at some dodgy artifact that Marcus was being coy about? Then so be it.

I landed at the airport around 4:30 AM, and Marcus was waiting to pick me up. He was a shorter man, with long blonde hair that made him look more like a surfer than a geologist, and for some reason sunglasses were perched on his head even though the sun hadn't even begun to peek through the windows of the terminal yet. He gave me a firm handshake and we walked together to the car. Once my bag was in the bed of his pick-up truck, I slid in the passenger seat, buckled myself in, and the very moment the doors were closed I turned to Marcus. "Alright, now what's so important that you couldn't talk about it on the phone?"

He laughed as he reversed out of the parking space and began making his way through the garage. "Business already, Alex? Come on, now, no questions on how your old friend has been?"

"We spoke a few months ago," I answered, feeling the irritation starting to bleed through my voice, "and so the only thing new in your life will have been whatever this thing is."

"Calm down, calm down," he soothed me, "I understand what the issue is. But I'm being serious, here, Alex. This is the find of the century. We're going to be mentioned in the same breath as Darwin if we play our cards right."

I furrowed my brow at that insane declaration. "Darwin. Have you gotten sunstroke?"

"I thought so, when I first found it!" Marcus grinned, turning his head to look at me. "But no, it's real as can be."

"Then what is it?" I snapped, my frustration finally bubbling over.

Sighing, Marcus came to a stop at a red light. "I'm trying not to tell you because you're gonna think I'm crazy."

"I already do," I remarked waspishly, only for him to continue.

"I thought I was crazy until I touched the damn thing, and I still have to pinch myself to be sure I'm not dreaming. I want you to see it in person, and you'll understand everything. Just gotta trust me for a few more hours yet. You hungry? Wanna stop by a drive-through?"

"...Sure," I answered, and left it at that for the moment. After we stopped for food, we drove out into the desert, taking the freeway south of the city. Those hours driving were suffused with nervous energy. I knew there was something out there that could possibly change everything, but had no idea what it was, and with every mile the car raced toward it, I found myself getting more excited and anxious, until my leg was frantically bouncing even as I placed a hand on my knee and tried to stop it. An old, childish nervous habit, one that I thought I'd long suppressed.

By the time we turned off-road and trundled down miles of dirt track, I was fidgeting in my seat like a nervous schoolboy, and let out an audible sigh of relief when I saw the barracks and parked cars in the distance. Pulling up alongside it, I leaped out of the car and turned to Marcus. "Alright. Now show me where this thing is, or I'll start to get upset."

"David's this way," he said, gesturing at me to follow him. I did, and glanced from side to side at the work-site. Men and women alike were sitting under the awnings, getting out of the Arizona heat, playing cards or drinking water, the low murmur of conversation falling silent as I passed, the employees looking at the newcomer as I made my way through the camp alongside Marcus. They seemed restless, none of them sitting still, even as their eyes were focused on me and me alone.

"They're all still here?" I asked, and he nodded.

"Paying them an extra two thousand a day to stay here and not blab. It's working so far, but I wanted you here quick as possible because… well, someone's gonna start talking sooner or later, and the fellas are getting pretty antsy!" We emerged out the other side of the camp quickly, and he directed me to a cave cut into the rock face of a mesa. "David's in here," Marcus said quietly, like we were in a library. "We were just doing some basic geological testing when we found him. Couldn't believe my eyes. Knew I had to get you."

I stepped inside the cave, the shade immediately cooling me off. I wiped the sweat from my brow, and looked around, as my eyes adjusted. Then my breath caught in my throat, and I had to remind myself to breathe. In front of me were the bones of a hand. I recognized it from anatomy, could clearly pick out the carpals, the metacarpals, and the phalanges. It was a left hand, spread out palm down against the dirt of the Arizona cave. And the proximal phalanx of the left pinky finger—the length between the first joint and the knuckle—was as large as my arm from fingertip to shoulder.

My knees nearly buckled, and I staggered against the wall, looking with wide, uncomprehending eyes at the skeleton of a giant. I'm a tall man, over six feet, but I'd be completely enveloped in the palm of its hand. It looked like some model, some practical effect made by paper-mâché and plastic... but it was real. The bones were cold and smooth against my hand, and I only noticed that I had placed my palm against them at that very moment.

"David, I've started calling him," Marcus whispered. I flinched at how loud his voice seemed, even as low as it was. "Like David and Goliath, though the other way around. Don't suppose you archaeologists know about anything like this?"

I shook my head, wordlessly. They were bones. Real, legitimate bones that were God knows how old, sitting here in all defiance of conventional wisdom and scientific inquiry. Impossible, lacking any evidence but itself, and yet all too real. "This is... insane," I breathed. "How could we possibly be the first to discover something like this?"

"I've no idea," responded Marcus, as he walked up to stand by my side. "Now you understand why I wanted you here. Any idea how old these things are?"

I shook my head. "Bones take a few decades to either begin the process of fossilization or just break down into dust." I tapped the finger bone in front of me, before I began walking toward the giant's head. "So conventional wisdom would dictate that David has been dead anywhere from three months to fifty years."

"There was a surge of cryptid and UFO sightings, back in the 50's and 60's," Marcus pointed out, following me. "They might have been fake, sure, but with David… it's entirely possible that people just didn't talk about it, in case they weren't believed."

"I suppose," I said quietly. "But still… my god. You're right. This is going to put our names next to Darwin."

The following hours were spent conducting as much preliminary research on the skeleton as I could. David was 47.371 meters tall, with a wingspan of 49.201 meters, giving him a ratio of height to arm length similar to that of a human. His skeleton was remarkably similar to that of a human male's, merely sized up considerably. I was not able to find any bones that were different from the typical fake skeleton you'd find in a high-school biology class, though of course that does not mean David was biologically identical to a human being. His organs and flesh, after all, had long since decayed away. As for his age? I have no idea. I wasn't exactly able to take a sample and send it back to a lab. Like I told Marcus, bones become fossilized or decay after decades, so either David had died relatively recently or the material his bones were made of was something entirely different than the mineral composition of nearly all other bones on this planet. Either is a possibility. Anything is possible now that I know about David.

In any case, his pelvis and ribcage, when compared to a human skeleton, would seem to indicate David as male. I say *seem*, because the skeleton is all we have. After examining it and measuring it, I spent hours on my knees in the dirt and dust of that cave, looking for anything that I might be able to classify as a cultural signifier. I found nothing. No coins to pay the ferryman of the dead, no goods for the afterlife, not even scraps of cloth from a favorite blanket. One of the most important aspects of any culture is how they treat their dead, their funerary rites and how they approach the subject of a corpse. So as far as I can tell, either David died naked and alone, or his corpse was placed in this cave and abandoned without anything by its side. And that's the most damning thing. I don't know. I can't know. David is the only one of his kind, so far as I can tell, and he's told us nothing. Well, he's told *me* nothing.

Marcus was the leader of the dig. You know, now that I come to think about it, I never asked what he and his people were doing out there. He had his own room, one he let me share with an air mattress and sleeping bag. I'm still surprised I was able to sleep at all, with how energized I was about this discovery. A combination of jet lag and exhaustion from constant focus—trying to make sure I didn't miss a single thing while searching around David—made me tired enough that I was able to fall asleep after only a few minutes of tossing and turning.

I woke in the middle of the night, heart racing in my chest like I had just sprinted a full mile and sweating like a pig. Panting, I slipped out of the sleeping bag and stood up, and noticed that

Marcus was gone from his own mattress. I didn't think much of it, just figured I'd see him when I went to the bathroom. So I walked outside and made my way to the bathroom. It was eerily quiet. It was the middle of the night, sure, but there was no snoring, no shuffling of sheets. I still don't know whether to attribute it to luck, or that lizard part of my brain that knew instinctively that something was wrong, but I walked over to the door of one of the barracks and opened it. I have no idea what I was going to do if I had woken anyone up. Apologize, probably — lie and say I was looking for the bathroom. But I didn't wake anyone up. No one was there. The beds were empty, sheets and sleeping bags rumpled and thrown aside.

My first thought was that they had left. I imagined the workers had gotten sick of staying there, driving back to town to give the location and photographs to some news anchor, and robbing Marcus and I of our names in history. I spun on the spot, but all the trucks and vans were there, sitting silent and cold in the night. I counted them twice, but there were exactly as many there as there had been when I pulled up with Marcus the day before. So where were they?

Then, my second thought hit, and it was even more terrifying than the first. What if they were doing something to David? I was running before the thought even completed, bare feet pounding against the sandy dirt as I gasped for breath, never before having cursed my lack of athleticism like I did at that moment. I couldn't hear anything over my own breathing, over my heart pumping in my ears as I prayed as fervently as I ever had in my life for David to be intact, for him to not have been destroyed. And then I reached the entrance to the cave, looked inside, and had to physically stop myself from crying out, my hand slapping over my mouth as my eyes went wide.

Inside was what I could only describe as a silent riot. Men and women alike struggled and fought against each other in total silence, the only sounds being the impacts of flesh on flesh, of stone on bone, none of them grunting or crying out in pain. All were grappling with each other inside a perfect circle, with some kneeling by David outside of it. I watched in horror as a man dressed only in boxers grabbed the beard of a man in sweatpants and slammed his head against the ground, the sickening crack cutting through the night as blood splattered across the earth. He left his opponent twitching there upon the ground, and dropped to his knees facing David, holding his hands up before lowering his head. For a moment, he froze in silence, before he rose to his feet, stepped forward, and walked over to the skeleton. There, I finally noticed what had happened to David, and I stifled a scream. His femur was broken clean in half, bone marrow seeping from the center of the bone. *Bone marrow!* Despite the fact that David had been dead for God knows how long, it was still yellow and fresh as the gelatinous substance quivered in its place.

The man in boxers walked up to it, passing by other kneeling madmen, and reached out with both hands like he was receiving a medal, scooping a double handful of marrow into his hands, before burying his face in it and devouring it with messy smacks I could hear form the entrance of the cave. I couldn't move, couldn't breathe, as his hands pressed into his face, leaving streaks of marrow in his beard. His hands shot up into the air, and he screamed silently at the roof of the cave, veins standing out on his neck and muscles tense, even as not a sound left his lips. Then he collapsed to his knees, eyes half-lidded and flickering, and another victor walked up behind him, reaching out to imbibe in David's marrow.

They fought and struck and killed each other on that cave floor, and I watched for far longer than I should have, unable to tear my eyes away. Marcus, I saw, was dead on the ground, half of his skull crushed and shattered, the single eye left in his head staring sightlessly at the cave entrance—at me. The dirt became clumped and wet with blood and gore, and eventually there was none left but the victors, kneeling and twitching next to the shattered bone of David.

Once more, there was silence, and I began to move, slowly shifting my weight against the sand, desperate to not get the attention of the madmen in the cave. Then, there was movement. I froze, heart leaping into my throat, as one of the victors—an older man with salt and pepper hair who had been kneeling there since before I had begun to watch—rose to his feet. He staggered over into the ring of slaughter and waited there patiently. The man raised one hand in front of his face, staring at it, turning it back and forth. Then something began to move under his skin, and my eyes widened as a spike of serrated bone the size of a kitchen knife parted his flesh, sticking out from the joint where the wrist met the palm like some obscene talon. Turning his head, he looked at another victor, a woman who was now walking over to him. She raised her arms to him, and what I can only describe as teeth-like scales erupted from her arms, blood running over the white enamel as she stroked them, the sharp tips cutting her palm. Without any word or signal, the two launched at each other, beginning to fight with their mutated, horrific bodies, even as the other victors began to wake, stirring to consciousness with mutations of their own.

This was the point at which I knew I had to leave. Slowly, carefully, I backed down the hill, and once I could no longer see the people fighting inside the cave, once I could no longer hear the impacts of their blows, I sprang to my feet and sprinted for the room. Hands shaking, I frantically tore through Marcus' bag for the keys to the truck. I grabbed them from the outermost pocket, snatched my own bag—surprised I had the presence of mind to do so—and ran to the cars. Unlocking the door, I threw my bag in the passenger seat and started the truck. Before I could see if any of the mutated freaks had heard me, I drove away as fast as I could.

I don't know what you people did to them. I don't want to know how bad those mutations got with every mouthful of bone marrow they ate. I don't want to know anything else about David, either. I still see him in my nightmares, though. A giant with endlessly writhing flesh, like choppy waves at sea, with flotsam of bone and teeth bobbing to the surface as he encourages me, in a booming voice, to feast on his body and drink his marrow.

Written Testimonial of Alexander George Kinney, shortly before his suicide.

04

MOCKINGBIRD'S

There are, most of the time, several dozen, if not hundreds, of "magic" stores in a city.

Usually, they claim to be proficient in every form of fortune-telling known to man. They can read your palm or deal the tarot or look into a crystal ball and know your future with precision, even as they give proclamations that can be interpreted in a hundred different ways. Of course, they recommend purchasing overpriced quartz and glass charms from them to ward off some unspecified evil that is approaching rapidly. Their shops are covered from roof to floor in thick, heavy curtains and decorated with statuettes and charms, lit with candles and burning incense, the smell almost thick enough to choke.

One and all, they are charlatans. They hide their lack of knowledge behind props and costumes, vague declarations and overpriced objects that can be made in half an hour of work or picked up at the beach. Business for them comes in the form of the superstitious and the bored, those who think it could be fun to indulge in a little pagan ritual and let a fortune-teller mumble some nonsense, like how they did in the carnivals during the past century.

There is, most of the time, only a single store in a city that deals in true magic, true occultism. It is never one of those stores that proclaims loudly and proudly that here one may purchase a reading of the future, or a crystal suffused with energies. It is small and quiet, one that goes under the notice of the authorities by being one of a thousand other stores that do the exact same thing, such that it would be a waste of resources to fully investigate.

In Los Angeles, in 1996, that store was Mockingbird's. A bookstore that held nonfiction and fiction alike, new books and used. It took up nearly an entire floor of the building in which it resided and still was a veritable labyrinth, bookshelves creating passages barely wide enough for two people. Most people that came to purchase items there were the studious type, readers to the core who could get lost in the stacks for hours—the same people who could gladly spend all day at the library browsing. The others, however, were the true occultists of the city.

The proprietor of the establishment was Ms. Sparrow. I never learned her first name, even though I worked for her for just under eight years, and a part of me doubts it was her real name. She paid me in cash at the end of each week and provided me with a W-2 upon the onset of tax season each year. We might have been involved with the hidden sides of the world, but taxes were still as certain as death—more so, in some cases. I was the only employee of the bookstore, and rarely, if ever, did anything so mundane as organizing the bookshelves. Indeed, Ms. Sparrow took pride in how unorganized the entire store was, encouraging customers to drop their books wherever took their fancy. She abhorred the Dewey Decimal System with a passion, claiming that it had completely destroyed the romance of a bookstore, and after some years working in Mockingbird's, I came to agree.

She had, as I understand it, taken inventory exactly once, when she opened the store years ago, and instead kept a neat, handwritten list of sales in a leather-bound notebook by the cash register. At the end of each day, she would go through the receipts of the day, bound together by paperclip, and write each transaction down: a copy of *Dune*, sold for $4.99; a copy of *The Hobbit*, purchased for $3.99. It was a ritual she performed every day, and it was one she was often still performing by the time I left, taking my bicycle with me.

The occult dealings of Mockingbird's, however, were not put in that notebook. No, they were recorded in a different notebook, one that never left the back office where the paperwork and permits were kept. Those were far rarer. Maybe once or twice a week, someone would walk in and ask to speak with Ms. Sparrow directly. The first year I was employed there, I had no dealings with them. The second year, I was allowed to observe and learn, and the third, I was allowed to complete those transactions on my own.

They never paid in cash. The occult world, I have found, is one of barter and trade, and though occasionally these customers handed over golden coins that always felt warm to my hand as if they had been heated in a microwave, I never saw one with a credit card or bundle of bills in all the years I worked for Ms. Sparrow.

Once, in 1996, while I was observing the transactions, I saw one man, tall and thin, open his mouth and reach his entire hand and forearm into his throat. I nearly gagged as his hand, wrist, and elbow vanished into his mouth, before he pulled out a snake. It must have been ten feet long and as thick around as my thigh, with ivory-white scales patterned with scarlet-red ripples. The serpent lay there in his grasp as docile as a newborn kitten, as Ms. Sparrow retrieved a large reptile tank she had asked me to purchase with her card the previous day and placed it on the table in the center of the back room. I noticed then that the tank had been painted, thin lines of ink forming circles and geometric designs all over the glass. The man slowly, gently, lowered the creature into the tank, and closed the lid of netting. Suddenly, it seemed as if the creature woke up, and began to circle the tank, hissing as venom fell from its fangs.

In return, Ms. Sparrow walked over to the desk and retrieved a cardboard box, handing it to the man, who opened it and looked inside. In it was a set of four books, a silk pouch tied tightly with a drawstring, and a dagger about a foot and a half long—double-edged and rusted with what looked to be bloodstains. He closed the box and nodded at Ms. Sparrow.

"Thank you for your patronage of Mockingbird's, Mr. Taylor," she said, and nodded back.

That was, frankly speaking, a usual transaction between occultists. They exchange items that mean nothing to those who are not a part of their world, nod at each other, and go their separate ways once more. It remains an issue of incompatible philosophy, I think. A few months after Mr. Taylor had paid Ms. Sparrow in the form of a snake, I walked into the back room to find her reading a letter, fingers tracing over a white sheet of paper, flawless penmanship neatly covering the entire sheet, front and back, with lines of text.

"Is everything well, Ms. Sparrow?" I asked after a few moments of her not acknowledging me.

"Yes, Martin," she answered after a beat. Long seconds passed before she spoke again. "How long have you been working at Mockingbird's?"

"About… two and a half years, I think," I told her. "And about ten months since you started having me observe the… other transactions."

Slowly, she nodded. "I see. I have confidence in your ability to take care of the bookstore. Our other business, however… Do you think yourself able to take care of those, if I am gone for two weeks or so? I shall leave precise notes on who I am expecting, what they are purchasing and with what currency."

Furrowing my brow, I bit my lip. Most, I know, would have said yes regardless of whether or not they were ready. But I greatly respected Ms. Sparrow and appreciated my employment there, and did not wish to mess something up because I had thought myself able to handle the store when that wasn't the case. "I think so," I finally answered, and she smiled at me warmly.

"Are you sure? I truly mean it when I say I'd not hold it against you if you thought yourself unable to do so."

"I'm sure," I said, firmly this time. "I can do it. Where are you going?"

She was silent for some heartbeats and then spoke. "My sister has asked if I would be willing to visit her, out in England. It has been… quite some time since we last spoke. Letters between us come and go, and yet we barely ever speak of things that are significant. We tend to… quarrel. Multiple times over the years, we have very nearly killed each other. Such can be our disagreements at times. Once, she took issue with whom I supported to take the leadership of a certain cult after its leader died and so struck off my head and burned my flesh. For four years, I waited for the moths to fold themselves back into my flesh so I could move once more. Another time, I disagreed with her choice of hiding place for a secret item she was bound by oath to keep, and so severed her left and right halves, hiding them far away from each other until her paramour was able to retrieve them both. Still, she is my sister, and if she calls for me, I shall go. I will be leaving tonight on a flight. Could you take care of the front now, Martin? I need to write out instructions for you."

Stunned, I nodded and stepped out of the room. I had, long before this, harbored suspicions that Ms. Sparrow was not human. Nothing that could ever convince another, of course. Merely the realization that never once had I seen her blink or eat or drink, despite the fact that she was there in Mockingbird's from the moment I got there at eight o'clock in the morning to when I left at nine o'clock at night. Merely how she gazed upon a man who I swore stood over seven feet tall and was covered — shaved head to bare feet — in thin white scars ritualistically carved into his bronzed skin… and the scarred man lowered his head in deference and murmured a "By your will, Ms. Sparrow." Yet, she had so easily admitted it to me, and with such an absurd tale to start with.

Still, I had seen many things even before I had begun working at Mockingbird's, and even more afterward, so I simply accepted it. Eventually, after a few hours, she poked her head out from the back room, and asked me to come back in.

"These are the three transactions I am expecting over the next two weeks," she said, pointing at a sheet of paper she had pinned to the corkboard. "I have no concern about any of them. They are repeat customers and know better than to try to do anything to a representative of mine while I am gone." Ms. Sparrow lowered her finger, pointing at three cardboard boxes on the floor, each with a name written on it in her sharp, neat handwriting. "Simply take their payment and give them the box. Any additional information will be on the paper I've written for you. Should anyone else attempt to initiate a transaction, inform them the proprietor will be back at the beginning of the month. Understood?"

"Yes," I said, nodding my head. "Let them know that you'll be back at the beginning of the month, other than the three we're expecting." For a moment, Ms. Sparrow studied me, dark eyes boring into mine. My breath caught in my throat, and for a moment I was afraid she would shake her head and close the store for the duration of her trip. Slowly, she nodded, and reached out to pat my shoulder, once.

"Thank you," she told me, before nodding again, reaching into her purse, and pressing a wad of bills into my hand. "I shall be off, now. Your payment for this week and the next—the final week of my trip—you will receive on my return. Be safe, Martin." With that, she was gone.

The three customers that Ms. Sparrow was expecting were, as expected, no trouble at all. All three, I had spoken with or seen before, and so when they asked me where Ms. Sparrow was, they simply nodded in response to the explanation and continued on with our business.

The first one was the scarred man I had once seen Ms. Sparrow intimidate with nothing but a stare, who gave me a long-sword, pristine and shining, in exchange for his box. The second was a young woman with dark hair and a pretty smile, who when I asked for payment, shrugged off her shirt and took a hold of her right arm with her left hand. Then, she ripped it off, not a single drop of blood falling to the floor as she placed it on the table, my mouth hanging open as the girl took the heavy box in her lone remaining hand and walked out. The final one was a man dressed in the robes of a priest, a crucifix hanging from around his neck, who smiled warmly at me. He asked me about how I was finding Los Angeles and how Ms. Sparrow was treating me before he helped me move the wooden crate in his car from the street to the back room, then taking his box and leaving.

The problem came the final week Ms. Sparrow was gone. She was a tall woman, her black hair shot through with gray and eyes that were dull and flat as those of a dead fish, and she walked into

Mockingbird's with a briefcase and two men behind her. I stood up as she walked over, and she still towered over me.

"Welcome to Mockingbird's," I said. "How can I help you?" "This is Ms. Sparrow's establishment, correct?"

I blinked, somewhat taken aback by her bluntness. "It is," I cautiously answered. "How can—"

"I will be purchasing this place," she interrupted me, looking at me without any change of emotion on her face. "Name the price you desire." A rush of emotion went through me, and more than anything else, it was just confusion that echoed through my mind.

"I don't have the authority or ability to do that..." I trailed off, waiting for her to give her name, but the woman simply frowned.

"Yes, you do. You are here. She is not. If you are worried about her retribution, do not be. I can ensure you don't suffer the consequences."

For a long moment, I paused, my mind whirling about. Finally, I opened my mouth. "I think you should leave," I told her, trying to keep my voice firm as I could, as steady as I could. "I am not able to sell to you, and I wouldn't if I could. I don't believe you're welcome in Mockingbird's any longer."

The woman's face tightened, eyebrows furrowing. "That's the wonderful thing about Ms. Sparrow not currently being here," she almost spat. "I can convince you in different ways."

Looking back, she nodded at one of the large men behind her, who stepped forward as I scrambled backward—and he collapsed, boundlessly, to the ground.

There was dead silence in Mockingbird's for a moment, before there was a small rustling, like wind through leaves, and I saw a moth spiral up from the man on the floor. Had it been in his clothes? No—for a second came, then a third, and then I saw that the man's flesh was breaking up and transforming into the insects. Already, his left hand was almost gone, a cloud of moths with whispering wings hovering over the man. His chest still rose and fell, so he wasn't dead… but I certainly wouldn't like to be him, waking up.

We stared as inch by inch, the man's flesh fluttered away as moths, flying together in a slow cyclone above the steadily breathing man—a motion that stopped as his left chest began to fly away, his heart presumably vanishing into the moths above. At that, the woman clicked her tongue and turned to leave, walking directly toward the exit as the other man hurried behind, his once stone face now visibly panicked and nervous.

The moths of Ms. Sparrow—for I remembered her mentioning them, before she had left—didn't appreciate it, however, and fluttered forward in a burst of wings and antenna, a shout coming from the man before his entire body was lost in the cloud. There were no more sounds from him after that, and when the moths dispersed, there were not even clothes or bones left. He just vanished, as if he never existed.

"Those were costly investments." The tall woman's voice broke the silence with what is almost rage in her flat manner. "I will be remembering this and taking account, Ms. Sparrow."

For a moment, there was no response. And then a low, humming drone came from the moths, from the walls, the ceiling, the floor. I choked in horror as the wood under my feet began to twitch and unfold into an insect that fluttered up, its wings still the dark brown of the floor I had walked on every day for months now. Hundreds, thousands rose from every surface, the books and their shelves transforming themselves. Mockingbird's itself came to life and raised its hackles at the intruder.

She stared at the inside of the store, dragging those dead eyes across each and every inch, before stepping out and slamming the door. And just like that, the moths sank back into the floor and walls. The bookstore slowly returned to normal as I tried to shake the uncomfortable feeling that I had just been in the mouth of a beast ready to bite down.

05

HOLLYWOOD

I moved to Los Angeles when I was twenty-three, in the summer of '84. Like so many others, I had some vague desire to make it in Hollywood. That dream sucks in thousands each year like a moth to a flame. Thankfully, I managed to abandon it before it consumed me whole.

Not all are so lucky. They desperately flutter around even the dimmest of lights, chasing background roles in commercials, wordlessly smiling as brightly as they can at the camera in hopes that some nameless producer or casting agent will snap their fingers and lift them out of obscurity. It's a drug, just as bad as cocaine or heroin or meth in its own way. An addiction to the cold, unfeeling camera lens, to the theoretical world on the other side of it. And some people will do anything for another hit.

There are always people looking for roommates in Los Angeles, and so I found one before I even arrived in the city. Her name was Amber, a young woman a few years older than me. We laughed on the phone as we spoke about our shared desire to make it big, to be a star. She told me about a few commercials she had been in. That woman who bends down and smells the flowers before giving a radiant smile to the camera while the voice-over lists the side effects of some new pill. I was appropriately stunned and impressed, as only a girl from one of the small towns that dot America like zits could have been. Of course, everyone in Hollywood has appeared in one of those, at one point or another—a record of the lost and desperate.

In a way, I almost blame myself for it all. If I hadn't cheerfully gushed over what a big star she'd be someday, if I hadn't placed her upon some pedestal like the greatest of stars, would Amber have done everything that she did?

In any case, I moved in with her; the two of us shared an apartment in North Hollywood. I worked at a cafe, and on days off, joined that everlasting throng of young men and women going from audition to audition, lining up and offering ourselves to the impersonal eyes of the casting agents.

It's hard to say I regret it, even now, though. Even though I know what I do—how this industry eats people up and spits them back out—there was a glamour and excitement to it all. I likened it to drugs earlier, but that's not all. It was gambling, almost—gambling with fame and fortune and time, desperate to secure some role while in the middle of our youth and beauty and passion. It's hard to say I regret it, but of course, I do. It's a machine that devours the young, greasing the wheels of industry and art with the blood and sweat and tears of its victims. I can only be thankful I managed to drag myself out of it before too long.

Weeks turned into months, months dragged into a year, and soon I had been in Los Angeles for two years with only three commercial credits to my name. One night in late November, I left a casting call, script in hand. I looked at the line of hopefuls outside, waiting for their turn—some smiling, some stone-faced—and I over-heard someone talking about how excited they were. In that moment I saw myself, two more years down the line, only two more credits to my name. Another husk being drained of every last drop of my passion and youth... and I just left. I dumped the script in the bin, walked away, and decided never to audition again.

It didn't take long for Amber to notice, of course. The truth is, I was genuinely happier. It sounded like a betrayal. It felt like one, too, like I was abandoning some great cause we were both invested in. But it wasn't some great cause, was it? In the end, it was nothing more than the vague dream of a little girl who wanted to be a star, with no idea of the dedication or suffering it would take to get there. Regardless, she noticed I hadn't gone to an audition in a month. She curiously asked me one day while I was getting ready for work what parts I had read for, what agencies I had applied for. I told her the truth, thinking nothing much of it. I had stopped, and I felt good about it.

I still remember the look on her face, burned into my mind like a photograph. She was shaken to the core, like she had just been told there would never be another new actor or actress hired, ever again. Eyes wide open in shock, mouth slightly open, leaning on a chair to support herself. It was early in the morning, she had barely woken up, and her hair tumbled around her face in messy waves of black.

"Why, Cara?" she asked, stepping forward and grabbing one of my hands with both of hers. Amber was a small woman, shorter than me by a few inches, but the desperation and pleading in her eyes scared me a little. "Didn't you come here for this? Why are you giving up so soon? I don't understand…"

I shrugged nervously, eyes flicking over to the clock on the wall. "I'm just stopping for a while," I lied, and didn't even realize I had done so until a relieved smile crossed her face, and she dropped my hand. It hurt, a gentle ache that wasn't any more painful than my little brother wrapping his arm around me and squeezing playfully… but for some reason, it throbbed through my body, sending warning pulses from my fingertips to my toes. "I think I'll take a break for a few more weeks, just to keep myself fresh, right?"

Amber laughed a high-pitched sound that sounded more tense than usual. "Sounds like a plan, girl!" she giggled, taking a step back and reaching for the coffee pot. "I'm more of the… what's it called? Nose to the grindstone type, right? Just keep on going until I'm in! I'm getting better and better with each audition, you know. Getting past more and more rounds, until one day, I'm the only choice! I've almost secured a role in a new commercial, you know. One of those new weight loss drugs, I think, and it's not gonna be much, but one more thing on the list of credits, right? I think that you should keep on going, too, but if you need to take a break to be fresh, sounds good to me! You know, I…"

She continued to talk, rambling on and on as I slowly grabbed my bag and walked to the door, slipping on my shoes at the door mat. Amber poured her coffee and grabbed one of the many scripts that littered our small dining room table, reading it over and over again with a zealous fervor, eyes scanning it time and time again.

"Bye, Amber," I called. "Heading to work!"

There was no response, and I shut the door behind me. It might not be a surprise to know that many of those who worked at the cafes and restaurants in Los Angeles were also hopefuls to the acting industry. I heard from a coworker that Amber wasn't even making it past the first round anymore. That she hadn't for a while. Amber was desperate. She wanted the fame, the glitz and the glamour, so badly. She'd do almost anything for it. At the time, I just didn't understand what that meant.

After three more weeks, I told her I was stopping for good. I tried not to make a big deal about it, just letting her know I wasn't continuing with my efforts to make it in Hollywood. I was feeling so much happier, I told her, not constantly stressing about whether I was doing well in my auditions, about my inability to get cast. I liked my job and I liked the people I was working with, and in the end I just didn't want to keep doing it anymore.

She just stood there, in silence, not a single expression coming over her face. Her eyes… I don't want to read too much into things, even now. For three years, I knew Amber well. I saw her every day. She was my roommate and my friend, and I don't want to make her sound like someone who was crazy from the beginning. But those eyes… there was a burning jealousy in them. I think, in the end, she was envious that I had the strength to walk away from the light she so desperately craved, even though she was being burned by it. Devoured whole by the flame.

I found out what she was doing seven months after I quit going to auditions. By that time, I had been promoted to a shift manager at my cafe, and I was finding satisfaction in it. I made it home much earlier than I was supposed to. A water main had broken in the middle of the night and had completely wrecked the cafe. I went back, looking forward to an unexpected day off.

When I entered the apartment, the first thing I saw was a drop of blood on the floor. Crimson and circular, it stood out on the white tile. "Amber?" I called, raising my voice as my brow furrowed. "Is everything alright?" There was no response, just silence, as I quickly fumbled off my shoes, finally taking my eyes off the single drop of blood, only to see a trail of it leading further into our apartment. "Amber!" I shouted, leaving my bag to the side as I dashed forward, socks sliding on tile as I ran as fast as I could. My feet hit the trail, and I smeared the blood behind me as I sprinted to her room, flinging open the door as I panted.

The first thing I thought as I looked inside was that it was daylight. Things this awful weren't supposed to happen in the daylight, they were supposed to happen in the dead of night, with only the light of the stars illuminating the horror. But the daylight just exposed Amber all the more.

She looked at me with panic on her face, fear and hatred in her eyes, a pretty face half-distorted into a snarl. Half-distorted, because only half of it was showing. I don't know the name of the other woman. I remember her face, though, as vivid as the first movie I ever saw. She was tanned, with a dusting of freckles across her cheeks and nose, and half that face was sagging off of Amber's like a face mask. The other half was secured over the face of my roommate's, and was set in an easy, personable smile, despite the vicious expression on Amber's own. She was naked, apparently halfway from peeling the suit of skin off her own body, one half her own, the other half someone else. The hollow arm of the other woman was hanging like the sleeve of a sweater, swinging back and forth in the air conditioning.

I vomited. I couldn't help it, not with how the blood was smeared over Amber's skin and dripping on the floor, the face of that poor woman peeled off and dangling. Doubling over, I fell to my knees and wretched, only to cry out in pain as Amber screeched and charged into me, sending me tumbling back into the hallway and slamming against the wall. Air knocked out of my lungs, I looked up at Amber, and thought I was going to die. She stood over me, looking at me with her own eye full of rage, while the eye of the other woman sparkled with amusement and laughter. Opening her mouth, she tried to speak, but two voices tumbled out at once, each shouting and screaming and threatening.

Drops of blood fell from Amber's bare body as she rushed into the kitchen, flinging open the drawer and pulling a knife from it, before turning and taking a single, menacing step toward me. Then I almost sobbed as a loud knock landed on the door, with a shout. "Hey! Everything alright?"

"HELP!" I screamed as loud as I could, and the door burst open. A man maybe a decade older than I was entered and made eye contact with Amber.

"What the—" his shout was cut off as Amber screamed again, at the top of her lungs, and rushed toward me, knife in hand. I screwed my eyes tight, held up my hands, and desperately tried to ward her off—only to be buffeted by a small amount of air and hear the breaking of glass. Panting, I cracked one eye open, then the other, glancing to the side to see the window in Amber's room broken, blood smeared on the glass. Footsteps rang out on the tiled floor, and the man knelt next to me.

"Are you okay?" he asked worriedly. "I'm going to call the police. Do you need an ambulance?" I shook my head wordlessly, reaching out and grabbing onto his arms as he made the call.

The official report the police made, I learned eventually, was that a young woman, Amber Roche, attempted to stab herself and her roommate before fleeing through a window. Simple, clean, and elegant for a situation that was nothing of the sort. I know what I saw. That skin was attached to Amber like it was her own. That poor woman's face smiling with warmth, her eyes shining. The man saw it too, though the police didn't give his words any more credence than mine. I can't do anything about it, even though I know the truth.

Somewhere out there, in this city, is a woman who is attracted to the camera like a moth to a flame. And even if it rejects her, time and time again, she's so desperate for its love that she will inhabit others like a suit.

She will change her skin and face time and time again, leaving bodies in her wake as she attempts to fill the hole in her ego that will never be satisfied.

06
ZONE ROUGE

I've written this tale and burned it half a dozen times over the years. The first was a few days after it all came to an end. Before even a single week had passed, I threw the pages into the fireplace, writing it all off as unbelievable nonsense.

I could barely believe it, and yet I wanted to send it off to the government, to the scientists at an Ivy League, to those so-called occultists that pepper the corners of the world. I have no evidence but my word, and though I could swear up and down on the graves of my ancestors for generations… Well, they would not take my testimony seriously, and I have learned well what such things are worth, in the end.

But I have come to realize I cannot take this secret to the grave, so to speak. Dismiss this as the fantasies of a man stricken by grief, or as the scribblings of an amateur novelist. But I have come to realize that we pass away with nothing but our conscience, and I would not be satisfied before my God were I not to at least pass on my knowledge in some way. So, these writings are yours now, and whatever you do with them is between you and your conscience, just as how writing them was between me and mine.

It was the year of our Lord 1922, and although all American troops had been withdrawn from the European continent, I had elected to stay. It wasn't uncommon, in those days, to find a wife among the nurses there, and to either bring her back to America with you or to stay with them there. As for myself, a few years prior, a bullet had gone clean through my leg while I had served with the 4th Infantry Division, 47th Infantry Regiment, and so in France I stayed while my flesh healed.

There, I met a lovely young nurse by the name of Gabrielle, and though she was four years older, she accepted my overtures with grace and returned them in kind. By the time I was able to walk out of the field hospital under my own power in 1919, the war was two months over with and I had made up my mind to rent an apartment around Verdun to stay with her.

In 1920, we married, and she moved in with me, our small home filling up with joy the likes of which I had never known. In

1921, Gabrielle died in childbirth, alongside the stillborn daughter we had planned to name Amelie.

To this day, nigh upon 60 years later, I can hardly bear to think on that year, those horrible months following the passing of the love of my life and the babe who might have become the second. The two were buried together in a cemetery outside the city, and though friends wished me well and offered their support, my heart was in the casket that was even then being covered in dirt, marked by the headstone reading *Gabrielle Cooper: Loving Wife, Cherished Mother*.

I did not speak to my friends for several months after the death of my wife. If you have suffered a loss like mine, you are familiar with the malaise that wraps around your soul and mind, how even weeks later the wound in your heart opens all over again when you wake alone in bed, when you begin to call the name of your love before the word chokes your throat. Even now I languish on the pain! In any case, it took weeks before I felt well enough to venture out of my house—months before I was able to speak with my friends once more, though they were glad enough for my company.

There were two men I had befriended quickly in my years in France. The first was Matthieu Lorent, a man my age who had been in the same hospital as I for a brief period. I had been shot in the leg, as I previously said, and Matthieu had been likewise shot in the opposite leg, a fact which provided him no small sense of amusement. A shorter man with black hair that he had allowed to grow long after his discharge from the hospital and the service. He was ever laughing, and I do believe the only day I ever saw him without a smile was the day of the funeral. He was, in many respects, the one who kept me from following my love out of grief, and I cannot thank him enough for it.

The other man was six years our senior. His name was Louis Dupont, and though I try not to blame him for the events that followed—he was as ignorant as I—without him, I would not have been involved with any of it, so it is hard not to hold him at fault. He had once been a soldier in the French army, drafted into the forces when the Germans marched, yet in the first few months of the war had also taken a bullet in the leg. Unlike Matthieu or myself, he lacked the good fortune to have it pass straight through the meat. The bullet had shattered his femur, and the doctors had said it was a miracle the leg did not require amputation. Instead, he walked with a cane, teeth worrying into his lip as he grunted with each step he took.

Before the war, he had been a scholar of literary works, something both Matthieu and I lacked any experience with beyond the compulsory education provided to us. We were able to read, though we knew a few of our fellow soldiers could not, but we lacked the passion for it that Louis clearly had, and I can remember many a time where the man would gesture passion-ately as we sat at a table listening to him ramble on. Those are still times I fondly remember now, in my old age, having gone through another war since. Yet I've begun to stray a bit from the recounting of my tale. The fact is, it was through Louis that this whole thing began, and though I care for him yet, I cannot help but resent him for it.

In June of 1922, I finally was able to rouse myself from the throes of grief enough to visit the two of them in Verdun. The city was slowly being rebuilt from the shell that the bombings had turned it into, and the two shared an apartment in the thick of it. We met at one of the many cafes that dot the streets of France, and the very moment I laid eyes upon Matthieu he was out of his chair, rushing up to me and pulling me into a tight embrace.

"Thank God!" he exclaimed, ruffling my hair with one hand as the other remained tightly around my shoulders. "I worried I would see you floating down the street as a phantom rather than a man! You seem to be eating well enough, at least, which is always good to see. I do hope you aren't hunkered down in your apartment all the time and are talking to some folks. You cannot just sit there as if the mortar shells are falling!" The words streamed ceaselessly from Matthieu without pause, and frankly I was unable to thank him enough for it. Together, we walked back to the cafe, where Louis was sitting, and when I arrived there, he stood and gave me a quick embrace.

"I am glad to see you well," Louis told me, and I nearly wept from the sincerity in his voice.

"Thank you," I told him, "and you as well, Matthieu. I do believe you have kept me from passing of heartbreak."

Matthieu gave me a quick smile as he sat at the table. "Well, such is the duty of us wound brothers! Would be a damn shame for you to have survived Fritz's attempts on your life only to pass on after. Besides, the two of us are aware as well as you are that Gabrielle would be furious if you followed her so quickly."

The smile I returned to him was that strange one, that mingling of grief and joy you feel when one speaks fondly of the departed, both proud of their life and despairing that they are gone. "Of course," I murmured, "a regular Nightingale, she was."

We spoke for some time together about fellow soldiers we had met in the field hospital or in our unit, letters we had received from them and sent their way flowing in a constant stream that surely made the postal service rich men. The cafe owners must have been rich as well, with the amount of coffee and pastries the three of us purchased together, until eventually Matthieu begged off to head to his work, leaving Louis and I alone in a companionable silence.

It persisted for a good few minutes, the two of us enjoying our food and drink, before I noticed his brow furrowing, his hand kneading into his injured leg. Louis was never the type to wear his emotions on his sleeve. More times than not, he would simply dismiss any inquisition into his life, and we would move on.

"Louis," I spoke, "is everything well?"

He almost started, eyes flickering to me as if the man had forgotten we were sitting together. "What?" he murmured, before looking back down. "Yes, yes, all is..."

Most days, I would have taken him at his word and left it all be. But that day, perhaps it was because we had spoken of our friends who were suffering from shell shock back in their homes, perhaps it was because we had spoken of Gabrielle and her boundless compassion, or perhaps it was just fate. Either way, I pressed on.

"You don't need to be so aloof, Louis. Allow me to help you, just as you have done the same for me."

Sighing, he leaned his head back, looking up into the clear sky, beginning to swirl with reds and oranges as the sun set on the horizon. For a moment, there was silence between us, before he broke it. "I have received news from a friend of mine," he told me, almost reluctantly. "For years, I have known him to be a sober, rational man... and yet his recent letters have been closer to ravings than anything else."

"Shell shock affects us all," I said. "May God grant him peace."

Louis looked at me and gravely shook his head. "Julius did not serve on the front lines," he informed me. "He was an engineer, working to lay track and such. At the moment, he works relatively nearby—in the fields of Verdun, retrieving war materiel from the Zone Rouge. They say it will take hundreds of years for the area to become habitable again, so much artillery was fired upon the countryside."

"Hundreds?" I asked in shock, as Louis nodded. "I heard some were not allowed to return to their villages, but…"

"Such is what Julius tells me," he said, looking toward the horizon where those hills were. "I think that knowledge is taking a toll on him. It must be as if he were a worker on some great cathedral, knowing you shall die before your work is complete…"

I nodded but continued. "What… ravings is he speaking of in his letters?"

Louis frowned, glancing to the side and drumming his fingers on the table. "I…" he murmured, before shaking his head and letting out a heavy sigh. "Julius is a good man," he evaded, looking into his lap. "Though we are not as close as we once were, I hold him in high regard still. He is intelligent, compassionate… such rantings coming from him disturb me greatly. They are not his. Something has gripped him with such terror and fear that it makes me worry for him. It is as if someone else is writing with his hands and words. You should have no cause to think him a madman, for he is not, and yet these letters he has been sending me have taken such a turn for the crazed that it scares me."

Reaching out, I patted his hand in reassurance. "I am well aware of what emotion can do to the mind," I told him. "Gabrielle's passing still weighs on me heavily, and you are well aware what it did to me in those dark weeks immediately after. If fear me to judge him on that account, put it to the side."

For long moments, he was silent, before he sighed and looked back to me. "Julius claims that the dead are walking. That corpses rise in the Zone Rouge and roam the boundaries at night before dropping back down in the morning."

"I see," I said. "That… was something people in my unit who suffered from shell shock would say. That those slain by the artillery were coming back, either to protect their former brothers-in-arms or to take revenge because we were alive while they were not. And Julius is at the aftermath of the shelling," I continued, leaning back, "so I suppose it remains a possibility that the sight of it is sending him into hysterics?"

"I suppose," Louis sighed, closing his eyes. "I just worry for him. Were I to return home to the village of my youth and discover the priest there had renounced his faith and left for Russia to join the Bolsheviks, I would be less shocked than to find that Julius Gerard now believed in the dead rising again. Such tales should have been left in the ages of animal and witch trials."

"I agree wholeheartedly!" I laughed. "Now tell me, my friend, what else have you been doing at that library of yours?"

From there, the conversation idled this way and that, until finally we said our goodbyes and I left for my apartment. I had contemplated moving from it multiple times, but in the end I hadn't. There were memories there tainted by sadness and grief, but no bad ones. And in the end, I would rather keep the memory of Gabrielle than abandon her.

After I had been honorably discharged from the armed services due to my injury, I had secured a job at a nearby grocer. Perhaps not the most significant job in the world, but it paid well enough to allow me to live quite comfortably. The owner of the store, Mr. Solomon, was an elderly and understanding man who himself was a veteran of the Sino-French war, and so tended to pay me better and allow me more leeway than perhaps he should have—in between his long rambles about how if he was twenty years younger, he would have been right by my side firing artillery at the German advance. It was there I was working when Louis entered one Friday morning, visibly worried and clutching a piece of crumpled paper in his hands.

"Liam!" he called the moment the door was open by a mere crack, making me turn my head in shock at the familiar voice. The store was barely open, and yet here my friend was, earlier than even the regulars that came each and every day at the same hour.

"Louis?" I questioned, placing the meat I was wrapping down as Mr. Solomon poked his head out from the back room, bushy eyebrows furrowed in curiosity. "Is everything alright? Is Matthieu well?"

"Yes, yes," he answered, rushing up to me and spreading out the wrinkled paper on the counter. "Julius—the friend I spoke to you about some time ago—has taken a turn for the worse. His letters have become all the more incoherent, and the letter that I found today has… well, look!"

I did so and furrowed my brow. The handwriting on the letter was spidery and shaky, as if written in the throes of a seizure. Perhaps it was not unreadable, but it still took the work of moments to squint and read out the words on the paper.

I can bear the dead no longer, Louis. Goodbye.

So short and brief was the letter that I had read it twice before I understood it, glancing up to Louis in shock. "You think…"

"I do not know," he confessed, pacing back and forth in front of the counter, fingers worriedly clenching and loosening on his cane, his gait so uneven and fast that I was concerned that he would trip and hurt himself. "I would never have considered him a possible suicide, but these words… It is not like him, not in the least," Louis repeated. "I beg of you, Liam—would you check on him for me? I cannot, not with this damned leg of mine."

For a moment, I hesitated. I did not know Julius, but I knew Louis, and I did not believe I could rightfully call myself his friend if I failed to help him in his hour of need. For a moment, I imagined Gabrielle frowning, telling me it was my duty to help him, finger jabbing into my chest as we laid in bed together.

Blinking, I glanced back to the taller man and noticed the old soldier looking at me with desperation in his eyes and a pleading expression upon his face. Reaching out, I took the piece of paper and tucked it into my pocket.

"I can see him," I told Louis. "Making sure he is well is the least I can do for you, my friend." Reaching over the counter, the other man pulled me into a fierce embrace, which I returned, before letting go and staggering backward.

"Thank you, thank you," he repeated. "Julius would not do such a thing, I am sure of it, but… things I am sure would not happen seem to have been more and more common these last years." With that, he left, cane tapping against the wooden floor of the building as I looked back at Mr. Solomon, who was now at the counter by my side, a mild frown on his face as the door closed behind Louis.

"And what's this, now?" he asked, turning to me.

"Louis is a friend I met in the field hospital," I briefly explained to him. "An old friend of his is working in the Zone Rouge, and his letters have been worrying all receiving them. Louis is asking me to check on him, to ensure all is well."

My employer's face softened, and he grunted an acknowledgment. "Go see the man, then. God bless him. He defended the Republic and deserves better."

"Are you sure?" I felt compelled to ask. "I can wait until the next day, if—"

He waved me off, lowering himself into the wooden rocking chair he kept behind the counter. "Go help the poor man, for the love of God. I can man the shop well enough."

"If you insist," I said, taking my coat from the rack and

shrugging it on as I stepped out. "I will do my best to be back by tomorrow."

Grunting, Mr. Solomon waved to me as I left. My bicycle was against the wall, and I took it back to my own apartment, pedaling down the road past other pedestrians.

Wartime rationing of gasoline had eased up enough that I could drive to the Zone Rouge instead of taking my bicycle, but not enough that I saw any other people as I drove along the country roads. Once bumpy and filled with holes, now flattened by the constant procession of military vehicles—first French, then German, then French and Allied forces again, carving a path through the countryside that had formerly been so pristine.

For half an hour, I drove through the countryside, before coming to a stop as two young men in uniform rushed up to me from where they were standing on either side of the road, a wooden gate preventing me from driving any further. Beyond it, a complex of canvas tents trailed off into the horizon.

"Good morning, sir! I'm afraid I must ask you to leave. There are a great deal of artillery shells in the area yet to be detonated."

"I am aware," I said, turning off the engine and letting the sound die down. "I served before an honorable discharge due to injury. I have come to see Julius Gerard. He is a friend of a friend, you see, and—"

"Julius?" One of the men asked, interrupting me with concern in his voice. "You have heard already?"

"Heard what?" I asked, brow furrowing as I made to get out of the car. "A friend of mine received a concerning letter from him and asked me to see him."

"He vanished this morning," the soldier said, stepping back. "His cot was empty, and his tentmate claimed to have heard nothing in the middle of night. Julius' gear is still there as well, and—"

"That's enough!" the other man snapped at his compatriot, then glanced at me with an apologetic expression. "I will go get our commanding officer, and the two of you can speak then. For now, just wait here, if that's alright, sir."

I waved, before stepping out of the car and leaning against it. "More than fine, of course." He left, jogging into the complex of tents and leaving me with the other soldier, a man who uneasily shifted from side to side as we waited together in silence.

Sometime later, another man followed the soldier back from the camp to my car. The man, whom I assumed to be their commanding officer approached me, and I offered a salute to him after noticing his patches on his uniform. "Well met, sir," I greeted him. "Former Sergeant Liam Cooper, honorably discharged, at your service."

"Captain Emmanuel Clement, likewise," he brusquely greeted me. He was a tall man, with blonde hair cropped close to his head, and with an expressionless face. "I am told you have news of Julius Gerard?"

"News may not be the correct word," I told him, "but a friend of mine received a letter from him..." I handed to him the once crumpled sheet of paper, now neatly folded into fourths, and watched as his eyes scanned it, widened, and hardened.

Huffing, Clement folded it crisply once more and handed it back to me. "He was sending letters about his nightmares? How shameful."

"He spoke about them? My friend, Louis Dupont, thought it was quite unusual of him to be behaving like this."

"It was," Clement confirmed, "and I tried to speak to him about it. He was under my direct command—a very competent engineer, which is why I placed him in charge of the extraction of shells from the Zone Rouge. He knew when a shell was too dangerous to disturb and had to be detonated while still in the ground. I don't blame him for having the nightmares. God knows the day I sleep soundly again is far from today, but I tried to speak with him about it and he refused to do so. Claimed the dead were walking up and about—yet I've ever known him to be a wholly rational man." He paused for a moment, before sighing. "Were you in the infantry?"

"I was," I confirmed to him.

"Then you know how often you would find corpses everywhere," Clement said, voice low and distant. "How you would go over one trench and into another and find some poor bastard lying dead at the bottom, flesh bloated with time and disease, maggots and flies feasting on his flesh even as his clothing fuses with his skin."

"Yes," I answered quietly, my mind flashing back to those moments. "I do."

Every man who was in the Great War knows it. Those who suffered through the interminable days and weeks and months of trench warfare knew sights like that, and if they claim otherwise, I name them a liar. A liar with good intentions, perhaps, attempting to spare their children or grandchildren from the horrors of that war, but a liar nonetheless. And I was American, only entering the war some three years after it had begun.

For three years, the soldiers of every European nation had endured the trenches. I had my own share of horrific experiences in the mere year I served on the continent. I simply cannot imagine the plurality of horrors those other soldiers had experienced.

"Well, Julius wasn't on the front lines, or in the trenches," Clement explained.

I nodded. "Yes, Louis told me."

"I account him lucky for it," Clement continued, "and certainly have no blame for him—would that no man ever had to go in one of those damned things—but I do believe it might be that he simply has no experience seeing such things. There are corpses by the hundreds in the Zone Rouge, and they've been there for years now. For my part, I believe he merely has a weak stomach, which is no great failing."

"Entirely possible," I conceded. "But he's vanished, you say?"

"No," Clement said. "If he had, he'd be court martialed for desertion. Julius has merely gotten started early on his work in the Zone Rouge."

For a moment, I was puzzled, but nodded in agreement once I realized.

"Makes sense," I told him. "Would you mind if I took a walk?"

"Not at all," the captain said, and my opinion of him as a good man was firmly cemented. "I'll be taking my lunch here."

Nodding, I began to walk off into the camp. The two soldiers made to follow me, only to be stopped by a swift bark from Clement. The hustle and bustle of the army camp was one familiar to me; I had almost missed it in the years since my dismissal. It took mere moments to make my way through the camp, various servicemen looking at me and deciding it was none of their business what mine was. I came to the edge of the camp and slowed.

I stood at the edge of the camp for several long moments, looking out over the small hill the tents rested on. Slowly, I walked forward, boots pressing down on the green grass and small flowers of the French countryside until the soles of my shoes landed on mud. I came to a stop, and looked from side to side, where the greenery and vegetation came to an abrupt and sudden end, trailing off into dirt and muck. Then, finally, I forced myself to look forward, at the place where I and so many other men had hunkered down in trenches, praying that an artillery shell wouldn't come down on us like the wrath of God, ending our lives before we even knew what was happening. I looked out, once more, at the Zone Rouge.

There were no trees, no grass, no hint of life as far as the eye could see. It was merely an expanse of mud and holes, of abandoned trenches and impact craters, pillboxes and barbed wire dotting the landscape. Words cannot describe that odd transition, from life to nothingness, where nothing would be able to grow for hundreds of years due to the chemicals and metals that had leaked out into the soil, poisoning it for generations to come. It was like nothing on this earth, as if I had taken a step and ended up in Hell.

I thought, for a moment, of Dante, and remembered that the fifth circle of Hell was reserved for the wrathful, and it was described as a great pit of slime and mud in which men fought and tore at each other and suffocated under the muck. I wondered if one night, Dante had gone to sleep and seen the Zone Rouge from centuries in the past.

Not fifteen feet away from me, I saw the empty husk of a mortar shell, intact and half-buried in the muck. The writing on it was French. How many in that zone were French shells? American? German? British? Did it even matter when all had played a part in the utter destruction of what once had been a landscape so beautiful that France had long been the dream for all to visit one day? No, there was no blame in my heart for Julius, not while he had to watch his country and countrymen destroyed in front of his very eyes.

Taking a deep breath, I walked out into the Zone. The day was cloudy and overcast, and not a single ray of sun peeked through the clouds as my boots squelched in the mud, my hands slowly clenching and releasing as I glanced around. Being back here was causing my heart to race, my blood to pump. My body instinctively responded to a place I had spent months in, constantly under threats to my life. As I looked around, I could almost swear I was right back in the trenches, slogging through the sticky ground as mortars fell around me, as the crack of gunfire rang out.

A loud noise rang out at that very moment, and I threw myself to the ground as those wartime instincts took over, belly slapping into the mud and breath leaving my lungs as my mind scrabbled for where the shell might have landed, which compatriots of mine I would never see again but for their dog tags and torn limbs flung yards away from where they had once been standing. Gasping, I shot up, driving my hands into the cool mud.

Panting on my hands and knees, I glanced up. There were no men around me, no men in front of me. I was alone in the Zone Rouge, and that loud noise might have been a shell detonating, but it also might have been thunder. With that camp over the hill, I couldn't see the tents or hear the people anymore. I was alone in the hell on earth the armies of the world had created.

I kept walking, and once I thought I was far enough from camp, began calling out for Julius. Every minute or so, I shouted his name at the top of my lungs, and heard nothing in response, even as it became harder and harder to walk in the mud. The churned earth began disgorging more and more from its bowels. I saw a length of metal that seemed to me a destroyed artillery cannon, a helmet with a single massive and ragged hole torn through it, and a ripped uniform that lay in the grime. Hissing as my foot slammed into something, I bit my lip and glanced down. The shattered stock of a rifle was touching my boot, splinters coming off the wood and a finger—rotted to the bone, with maggots worming about inside the flesh—still curled about the trigger.

Swallowing, I closed my eyes, and tried to take a deep breath, but all I could taste was the tang of blood and the foulness of the air around me. Opening my eyes again, I turned around and looked for the hill upon which the military camp that presided over the Zone Rouge stood. I saw nothing, only a flat expanse of endless, shell-pounded mud, without a single spot of greenery in sight. Pillboxes made of wood and concrete stood broken and shattered like trees upon the landscape, while rusted barbed wire emerged from the muck like grass. Shells stood in the mud like tombstones, graves of the countless soldiers that had perished here, each one an unknown, the artillery shattering their bodies beyond all recognition.

"Julius!" I called again, and the word seemed to die in the still air. The air was still without even the slightest breeze, and the clouds overhead hung heavy with anticipation. No sunbeam broke the cloud cover, with no wind causing them to move. My brow furrowed.

There is an instinct soldiers learn to listen to after some time in the trenches, a sixth sense for the timing of artillery and gunshots, of gassings and firebombs—and it told me something was wrong. Something was strange, and it slid up my spine with a shiver that raised goosebumps upon my flesh. Another loud sound echoed around me, and I looked up at the sky. The clouds were gray and heavy, and fat droplets were beginning to fall, but there were no flashes of lightning. Whatever sound that was, it wasn't thunder. I looked down at my watch. It had barely been fifteen minutes since I had walked into the Zone Rouge. Huffing, I made up my mind to continue on. I had told Louis I would try, after all. I trudged onward.

I walked from one destroyed pillbox to the next. I looked down at my watch again. Three sixteen. Fifteen minutes since I had walked into the Zone. The second hand was still moving, and I watched, heart pounding and mouth strangely dry, as that long, thin piece of metal ticked all the way around the dial, and the minute hand refused to move. I knew the basics of how watches like the one around my wrist worked, how gears and springs could be wound together intricately into an elegant—and sometimes exceptionally expensive—piece of machinery. I knew something like this couldn't happen, and my blood ran cold.

"Julius!" I shouted again, and again the word died as soon as it left my lips. The rain was beginning to intensify, and my breath left my lips as steam. That's when I realized just how hot and humid it was. The rain fell like hot water from a shower upon my skin and sweat began to bead on my brow even as my breath misted like on a winter day.

"Julius!" My voice had the tinge of desperation to it now, and I struggled forward, pants so thoroughly stained with mud I knew in my core it would never come out. There were no more noises, and it was deathly silent, but for the patter of rain and my heavy breathing, my footsteps on the muck and the shifting of my clothes.

And then I heard it, the sound of someone else moving in the mud, and I whirled around with a thankful greeting on my lips— and froze in place. It was not Julius behind me. It was a corpse. A corpse that was moving, though it had but a single intact arm, and both of its legs were blown off at the knees, limbs ending in ragged stumps of flesh and bone. With that single arm, it reached forward, burying its fingers into the mud, and pulled itself along, in a motion so reminiscent of the crawl all soldiers are taught to perform that I felt myself grow lightheaded. A helmet adorned its head, but the ragged hole in it showed just how well the protection had availed the poor man, the sharp edges of the metal digging into the grayish matter of the corpse's brain and the stained white of its cranium, and I nearly vomited as I heard the sharp crack of the skull separating from the pressing metal. Maggots white as snow were living in the corpse's gray flesh, wriggling in and out even as it moved, falling to the pitch-black muck before squirming either back onto the corpse's body or worming their way into the ground. And then, it paused. A single glassy eye darted and looked directly at me.

No amount of alcohol nor laudanum has ever stripped that sight from my mind, and it has ever been the last thing I see before sleep each night. A corpse should not move. I say that as if it is not an obvious thing, but as it crawled up to me, that was the only thought in my mind. A corpse cannot move. Its muscles have broken down, decayed by time and eaten by insects. There is no life in the brain, no soul to inhabit the body. It has fled, God willing, to heaven, and will live there in paradise. And yet it moved, crawling through the mud and looking at me, even as a maggot fatter than my finger fell from the empty eye socket in its skull.

For a long minute, I froze. I wanted to flee, but my legs would not move. I wanted to look away, but my eyes could not tear themselves away from the dead man moving, the proof that Julius was not mad or a suicide, but that something unearthly was here in the Zone Rouge.

A glint reflected off something in the edge of my vision, and my eyes finally flicked down to it. A chain hung around the neck of the corpse, and I immediately realized what it was. Dog tags. Slowly, I bent down, kneeling before the moving corpse in the muck. With trembling fingers, I reached out and lifted the necklace from the dirt, the metal discs softly jingling against each other as they hung in the air. With the other hand, I reached out and scrubbed off the dirt with my sleeve.

There were letters on it, but for the life of me I couldn't read them. They weren't Cyrillic or Greek characters, nor were they the logographs of the Asian languages. Were the letters Roman? It would seem to be the case by process of elimination, and yet every time I've tried over the years to copy those things onto paper, it seems to come out differently. In the end, would it even matter if I knew the name of the man who had once inhabited that poor corpse? He remains dead and gone, after all.

Letting the discs fall from my hand, they swung back and forth, and I stepped back, looking at the corpse still. Once I was a few paces away from the poor thing, it broke eye contact with me, and began once more crawling across the land. I remained frozen as it crawled over a small rise and vanished from sight. Suddenly free once more, I scrambled to the top of that hill in a burst of motion—and found that it was gone.

Another sound caught my attention, and I glanced to my left to see a second corpse, this one with both legs intact. Its sole arm was grasped tightly to its weapon, finger inside the trigger guard, using it as a cane to support its weight as it staggered on. The stock was wooden, but I couldn't recognize the gun. The metal was coated with grime and dust, scratches up the barrel holding dirt and a twig stuck in the chamber. The thing walked past me, trundling on until it entered the remains of a bombed-out pillbox and vanished from sight.

I didn't call out for Julius anymore. In fact, at that exact moment, I made up my mind to leave. Perhaps it is strange I refused to flee at first, but I think there was yet a part of me that tried to deny what I was seeing, an attempt to convince myself I was hallucinating visions from the leaking chemicals, or a resurgence of my shell shock. But there was no way to deny the cool metal dog-tags on my fingers, the sounds of maggots falling into the mud. I should like to say that I left with tears on my cheeks and a prayer in my heart for Julius, who I had now realized was lost to whatever was happening in the Zone Rouge, but the truth is I did not consider him at all. I just knew to my bones I had to escape.

I turned around and began walking as fast as I could against the sucking muck and mud, struggling through it as I walked over rises, past tangles of barbed wire and shattered remnants of artillery. Once more, I glanced down at my watch, despite knowing what I'd see. The device on my wrist claimed it had been fifteen minutes since I had walked into the Zone Rouge. And so, I kept walking.

I tried keeping track of time by counting the seconds, but I lost track too easily, starting at each noise that seemed to shatter the still air, interrupting the hot rain. Eventually, I tried to keep my spirits up by humming a song, but I stopped after just a few bars, a shiver running up my spine. So, the tune died on my lips, and I continued to walk, endlessly, into the gray horizon.

I walked for what seemed like hours. My legs burned, my feet were soaked, and the heavy clouds ahead never moved or swirled, simply continuing to rain on the muddy fields of the Zone Rouge. What I saw blends together into a morass of hell on earth. I saw a pillbox stuffed to the brim with corpses, their jaws opening and closing as if they were still alive, so twisted together that I was unsure if they would ever be able to get out. One corpse was so deep in the muck that I stepped on his ribcage, only aware he was there when my foot suddenly sank deeper with a crack of bone and that horrible, meaty sound of flesh parting from flesh that only those who served could ever know.

The most intact one I saw had all their limbs intact, and was slowly, relentlessly, deepening one of the trenches with its shovel, even as the mud kept slipping back into place. I stopped to watch him for a minute or two, consumed by my own memories of the same action, digging deeper and deeper into the dirt as the mortars fired and officers shouted. Now, though, the world was silent but for the raindrops, and every slam of the shovel into earth felt like a gunshot.

Suddenly, I was struck by the sudden urge to attempt to talk with it. I took a single step forward, almost unconsciously, and the corpse stopped moving, shovel buried in the dirt. Slowly, it turned its head, black hair hanging lank over its face as it looked directly at me with glassy, unseeing eyes. We stared at each other, man and flesh, for a moment, before I opened my dry lips.

"Hello," I said, the word sounding unnatural to my own ears. It didn't reply. Rainwater pooled in the divots where its flesh had been eaten or torn away, overflowing as it stood motionless before me. I took one more step forward, and nothing happened. We were standing face to face, now. Its uniform was not one I recognized, but the color was reminiscent of the German infantry, the pockets in the same layout as the French. Those dog tags rested on his chest, glimmering in the gray light. I stepped back, and once I was about a yard away, it began to dig again, going through the motions of making a trench for a war that was not yet over in its flesh.

I walked away and kept walking. What else could I have done? It was dead, and yet it moved. The soul long fled, the brain active no longer, yet something else kept it moving. I could have destroyed the body somehow, broken bones with the twisted metal around, but such a thing felt like blasphemy and desecration, and I don't believe I could ever have brought myself to do such a thing, even without the consideration of it defending itself against me.

That may have been the most intact corpse I saw, but it was certainly not the last. Some crawled, some walked, some dug, some built, and some just laid there in silence such that I was not sure whether they were in motion like the others, or true cadavers that had found their way into this hellscape. It felt like I was walking for hours. I might have been. But either way, I was in a daze when I took another step forward and my feet fell onto grass. I looked back at where the Zone was, that dividing line of green grass and tamped dirt, and glanced down at my watch. It ticked over to seventeen minutes past.

It has been many, many years since that day in the Zone Rouge, when I walked into something that was not of this earth, and by the grace of God was able to walk back out again. Julius was not so lucky. He was never found, and was listed as a deserter, though most thought he took his own life out there in the Zone. I think he found his way to that strange space and was never able to find his way out again. I have no idea what allowed me to leave when he did not. Was it because I had seen combat? Because I spoke to that digging corpse? I do not know, and I have never gone back to that place again.

I have never told anyone about this. About the corpses that walked like men, about the language on the dog tags I did not recognize, about how that place was larger than the Zone Rouge itself. No one would believe me, and if they did, how many would say it was my shell shock, or the chemicals that leaked from the shells causing me to see things that were never there?

In the end, however, I think they might be the closest thing to right. The Zone Rouge, it is said, will take hundreds of years to be inhabitable once again. Chemicals have leaked into the ground, heavy metals have poisoned the earth, and gas has soaked the dirt. What else might have leaked into the soil from those years of hard bombardment?

Despair, perhaps. The quiet terror of knowing at any moment you might die from a mortar shell. The desperate and terrible emotions of thousands upon thousands of men who died, fear in their bodies and screams on their lips, staining the earth with their agony and terror. And now that the factories of men can produce death and its implements in such great quantities… where else on this earth might be soaked in human suffering to such a degree?

ALPHONSE SCHALLER

07
THE UNLUCKY

There are always people going missing in the national parks. Most go in, then come out none the worse for wear, having enjoyed a pleasant trip and a weekend away from the urban sprawl humanity is so good at creating. Some, however, fail to make it back.

Poor preparation is the cause of most of those. Failing to bring the right clothing or reading the map wrong, willfully disregarding the warnings of those more experienced than themselves and passing as a result. Some die as a result of weather, animals, or freak accidents that not even the most experienced backpackers could have seen coming. The rest, we call the *unlucky*.

Once you've been in the Forest Service for long enough, you know what it means when another searcher says whoever we're looking for is *unlucky*. It means something weird got them, one of those things we don't talk about outside of work because no one would ever believe us. But anyone who's spent a few weeks away from the cities in those forests can tell you: there are things in the woods that don't much care for whether or not you believe in them. Especially in Appalachia. Those mountains and woods are some of the oldest in the world, and it's downright arrogant to think we know everything about them.

The point is this: if someone comes back and says the poor bastard got *unlucky*, it means nod your head and move on. If we're fortunate, we might find their corpse—or parts of it—in a few months or a year. If we're not, we'll find them alive.

We found one alive ten or eleven years ago now. A seven-year-old kid named Madeline went missing in the forest, and the parents were devastated when they called us. I wasn't the one who took the call, but a buddy of mine did, and he said they could barely get a word out through the sobs. Swore up and down that they only looked away for a moment, that she was a good girl who wouldn't wander off. That they had been calling for her for hours and that she knew if she got lost, she was to stay in place.

I was part of the crew looking for her, but we didn't find anything. Well, that's not true; we found her backpack. It was bright pink, had a water bottle and a granola bar in it, and had been wadded up and shoved under a boulder. That was the point at which we knew we weren't going to find her. The point at which we knew she was *unlucky* as opposed to just being grabbed by some creep was when we found her shoes. They were hers; her parents confirmed it when we showed them the photo we took. She had been wearing little sneakers with Disney princesses on them, and they had been neatly placed side-by-side on the doorstep of the girl's bathroom at the entrance to the park, socks balled up and put inside.

That's the type of thing that we mean when we say that someone was *unlucky*. Weird, unexplained things like that. Once, we found a guy who had been separated at each joint. Not torn apart, like some animal had gotten him, but cut, clean and precise, at each joint in his body—finger joints, toe joints, the wrists and elbows and shoulders and knees and ankles. It wasn't a pleasant sight. Another time, we found a kid that had been missing for months curled up in a cave. He had been dead for only a day or two, said the coroner, and apparently had cooked food in his stomach. *Unlucky*, both of them.

But this time, we found the girl alive. One day, about four months after she vanished, she walked right out of the woods and up to the desk at the visitor center. I was the first officer called in, and I remember just how much of a shock it was. I recognized her face right away, of course. I don't think many SAR personnel forget the *unlucky* ones—especially the kids. Bad enough for things like that to happen to an adult... but a kid? Heartbreaking.

The first time I saw Maddie Cooper in person, she was swinging her feet back and forth on the bench, eating a granola bar as the greeter at the desk looked at her nervously, glancing away to try to stop himself from staring. When he saw me, he practically leaped out from behind the desk and ran up to me.

"Thank God you're here, Jacob," he murmured, voice low. "I'm not wrong, am I? That's that girl that went missing a few months ago?"

"No," I answered, looking at her. "You're not."

At the time, I had been with Search and Rescue for only five or six years, so I didn't know enough at the time to be nervous or afraid. I should have been, but that's on me, in the end. I walked up to her and kneeled, looking forward at her. Maddie was wearing the exact same thing she had been in the photos her parents had given her: a pink jacket, beige shorts, with her blonde hair tied up in a ponytail. We had put that photo up on a wall in the SAR offices—a quiet little memorial to everyone who had been *unlucky* in our park.

She looked at me and smiled. "Hi," Maddie said, before taking another bite of her granola bar.

"Hi," I echoed back to her. "I'm Jacob. Do you remember who you are?"

"Of course!" She smiled. "I'm Maddie Cooper."

"That's good," I said, keeping my voice low and level. "You've been missing for a long time, Maddie. Can you tell me the last thing you remember about the day you were with your parents?"

For a few moments, she was silent, face smoothing out and looking thoughtful, as she stared into the middle distance. "I remember going on a hike with mom and dad," Maddie eventually said. "I remember having lunch. I remember… I saw a fox or something. And I followed it!"

I nodded. "Got it. Do you remember who you've been with all this time?"

She shook her head. "Nope." For some reason, at that moment, I felt a chill run up my spine. And I knew, deep down in my core, she was lying.

"Okay," I said cautiously, not wanting to push any further. As someone who might be the first person to come into contact with a missing and traumatized child, all SAR members are trained to speak gently and delicately with children. But she had lied to me, I knew in my gut, and I no longer felt comfortable speaking with her. "I'm going to call the police and get them over here so we can get you back to your parents, alright?"

Her eyes flickered back to me, and she smiled as I rose to my feet. "Okay! Thanks, mister."

I returned the smile as best I could, then called the police. I remember their long embrace, the sobbing of mother and father alike, but Maddie herself didn't seem all that affected. I just kept remembering how she lied right to my face, even as the Coopers and the police filed out of the visitor center, and as I walked to the office to take her off the wall now that she'd been found. I heard a voice from behind me as my fingers touched her photo.

"What are ya up to, Jacob?"

I turned to the man behind me, a grizzled old veteran by the name of Arthur. "Arthur," I greeted him. "Maddie was here. Walked out of the woods and into the visitor center. Thank God she's safe, huh? I'm taking her off the wall…" My voice trailed off as I continued, eventually going silent.

Arthur had been with Search and Rescue for a few decades, ever since he left the army, and was by far the most experienced member of the team. So, to see genuine worry and concern on his face at what should have been good, happy news unnerved me. "Everything alright?"

"Sure it was her?" he asked.

"Yeah," I responded. "Everything okay?"

"No," Arthur said brusquely. "No, it damn well isn't."

"We got a girl back," I argued, furrowing my brow in confusion. "That's worth celebration, and why on earth would you think otherwise?"

"Because she's one of the *unlucky* ones," he answered me, before sighing. "Come on. Follow me."

Without complaining, I followed the more experienced man through the hallways to a meeting room with door ajar. Together, we slipped inside, then Arthur shut the door behind us before turning back to me.

"Well, where to start?" Sitting down on one of the chairs, he leaned back, letting his eyes flutter almost closed.

"How about why you're upset a little girl came back alive?"

Slowly, Arthur shook his head. "It ain't about that, Jacob. How long have you been with Search and Rescue?"

I sat down, relaxing back into the chair. "Five, six years now."

"So, you've gotten the chance to see a bunch of *unlucky* ones, right? Usually get about five, six a year. You know how long I've been in SAR? Twenty-nine years last October. Know how many times I've seen an *unlucky* person show back up? Twice. And both of them… they weren't right, once they got back.

"The first was back in '80, a father by the name of Victor Adams. Ducked behind a tree to take a leak and vanished. Found his clothes at the top of a tree, nearly thirty feet up, about a week later and twenty miles away from where he vanished. No blood on them or anything. Pretty standard, far as *unlucky* people go. Then he got found, about a month and a half later, asleep in a lake, just lying on his back, floating there without any clothes on. On the other side of the damn country, mind you. Family had questions, obviously, but he claimed to not remember anything, and the doctor's examination didn't turn up anything unusual, last I heard, so they didn't push too deep. Just happy to have their dad back. At the time, there was an old-timer on the SAR, Chuck, and he told me just what I'm telling ya now. That when people come back from being *unlucky*, that's worse than if they don't come back at all. It was true for Victor Adams, that much is for sure.

"Got hushed up by the cops because no one wanted all the details to get out, but they came to talk to us after it was all over. Wanted to double check everything we said about him having vanished for so long. See, he wound up skinning things. Squirrels, first, and started using their skins to make a life-sized figure. Worked his way up, too: cats, foxes, dogs. Eventually killed his family and used them to make some sort of skin-doll, may they rest in peace and that bastard burn in Hell. Caught him after he tried to grab someone from outside his family, searched his house, and found that… doll. Ended up having to shoot him dead after he attacked them is what I heard, though I don't think anyone was particularly sorry to see the last of him. Tossed the skin-doll in an incinerator, and that was the end of that. People working the incinerator had nightmares for ages, though – swore that they could hear the thing screaming the whole while.

"Second one was in '92, a young woman by the name of Janice Weathers. She went missing during a camping trip. Her friends and boyfriend woke up and she was gone. Clothes were all in place, pack was still inside the tent and her shoes outside the flap—looking like for all the world she just walked out of her tent in her sleeping clothes. Dogs tracked her scent in five different directions, and that's when we knew she was an *unlucky* one. Boyfriend was beside himself, her family as well. She had an older brother who had recently left the army, and he was out here with me near every damn day looking for her. About three months in, another group of SAR members found her in this forest, about three miles from the visitor center. Which made no damn sense – that section of the park had been checked about a dozen times over, but since when has making sense ever mattered to those poor *unlucky* bastards? Everyone was overjoyed, but just like Victor, she didn't remember a thing.

"About a year after Janice was rescued, she got pregnant by her boyfriend, and they chose to have a quick wedding. Nothing particularly scandalous, but there were still a few old folks huffing about it. I had gotten to be close friends with her older brother, and from what I understand, the pregnancy was more or less normal. Cravings, the baby kicking, all that sort of thing. Then I get her brother calling me, yelling at the top of his lungs about some abomination that she gave birth to. Try to calm him down, but he's absolutely losing it. Couldn't get much out of him that night, but he eventually showed me a photo of the kid. It had the head of a goddamn deer, Jacob. Dunno what happened to her after that. Her brother sure didn't wanna talk about it afterward, and that entire family just pretended she didn't exist.

"So that's what happened the last two times someone who was *unlucky* came back from their disappearance. That's why I'm not too excited about this girl coming back alive. Sometimes, death can be a better fate than something else that's in store."

Frankly speaking, I don't think I took that warning as seriously as I should have. But even if I did, what could I have done? Say to Arthur I was certain she was lying about not remembering who she had been with all that time, told the police to take her away, lock her up? No, there was nothing that anyone could have done at that point save take a gun and shoot Maddie Cooper, and I have my doubts whether or not that would have worked, even so early on. Because Maddie Cooper was changing, slowly but surely.

The next summer, she showed up again. I was at the front desk, and blinked in astonishment as I saw her walk through the front doors of the visitor center.

"Hi, mister!" she chirped, raising her hand to wave to me. Her parents walked in behind her, clearly nervous. I didn't blame them—I would be too, if my kid was in the same place that they had vanished in not a year before. She had grown taller, and her hair was now tied back into a single ponytail. "You talked to me when I came back, right?"

"I did, Maddie," I said, turning to her. "It's great to see you again. How are you?"

"Good!" Maddie answered, smiling. "I wanted to come back and explore some more!"

I flicked my gaze to her parents, who shifted nervously behind her. "Glad you're excited, sweetie," her mom said. "Come on, let's wait outside for dad to get a map, alright?"

Maddie nodded in agreement, then hummed as they walked outside, her father stepping up to me. "Sorry," he apologized. "She was just so insistent on coming back..."

"Why?"

He shook his head slowly. "I don't know. The counselor said this would be good for her, though, so here we are. It makes me nervous, though."

"I understand why," I said to him. "Don't let go of her hand, huh?"

He laughed, short and sharp. "That's the plan, certainly." Grabbing a map from the visitor center, he left, and I watched as the family walked away.

The next summer, they were back again, and Maddie eagerly told me about how she wanted to work in the forest when she grew up and got older. She sprouted like a weed, and by the time she was in high-school, she was nearly as tall as I was—and I'm not a short man. By that time, her parents had long since accepted that she was no longer at risk of suddenly vanishing from their sight as she once had. They were far more indulgent of her willingness to run off into the woods, hiking on her own for a few hours at a time before returning to her campsite.

I have no idea why she told me all this. Maybe she recognized I knew she had lied, or maybe she had just become genuinely attached to me. No matter what, though, it all came to a head when someone else went missing while she was in the park.

I was looking through the park alongside another guy by the name of Nolan. It was past sunset, and our flashlights swept across the dark trees, reality almost ceasing to exist outside the circles of light they provided. I thought I heard something through the forest and stopped dead in my tracks.

"Do you hear that?" I asked Nolan, and he paused as well. It sounded like an animal, snuffling and chewing.

"Yeah, I do," he answered—but not quietly enough, apparently, because the sound stopped almost immediately.

I held a hand up and together and we slowly walked forward. Twigs crunched under our boots, and for a moment, it felt like the whole world was holding its breath. Then there was a sudden surge of movement, and I yelled, swinging out blindly as Nolan was taken to the ground. I fell, feeling the wind leave my body as my back hit the ground harder than I had ever fallen before. As I lost my breath, I heard Nolan scream at the top of his lungs—a scream which cut out with a gurgle of blood and gore.

"NOLAN!" I cried with burning lungs. I rolled over only to see someone hunched over him, claws glimmering red with blood in the brilliant light. A single hand lifted an unidentifiable handful of meat, before letting it fall, disappearing into the gullet of the beast, leaving a stain of red on Maddie Cooper's face.

Looking back at me, she grinned, and I remember every detail. Her teeth were long and sharp, made for slicing and tearing through meat. Those hands were tipped in razor-sharp claws, and her forearms bristled with gray fur. Yellow and slitted, her eyes shone in the darkness like those of a predator.

Even as I watched, I saw her twitch and shake, veins bulging in her neck and arms as she grew in size, her hair lengthening and muscles growing. Reaching down, she buried her hand into Nolan's chest, and pulled out his heart, unceremoniously beginning to devour it as I yelled out in horror, grabbing a nearby branch and flinging it at her with all the strength that I could muster.

It wasn't enough, though. It smashed in the side of her head but barely caused the girl to flinch. Instead, she just laughed—a strange, guttural thing—then flung it right back at me. My stomach buckled around the blow, and I collapsed to my knees, feeling blood rise through my throat and out my lips. By the time I looked up again, Maddie Cooper was gone.

Officially, she was listed as another disappearance. Unofficially, I told everyone not to look for her, not to do anything to her if they saw her. Arthur just clapped my shoulder and sighed, reminding me what he had said about the *unlucky* ones coming back.

Nolan wasn't the only one found dead in the park. The missing person we were looking for was found dead as well, with bite and claw marks all around her body—the same ones on Nolan, and the same ones that have been found on wolves, bears, and foxes in the park ever since. But honestly, what I fear the most is the day those corpses stop showing up and Maddie Cooper moves on to hunt elsewhere.

08
PLAYTHING

It's following me, that hideous beast with its slavering tongue! It wants nothing more than my flesh, and nothing can appease its hunger. Every creak in this damned hotel, every brush of the wind against the window, it all makes me twitch and jump, even as I write—each a sign of that damned beast coming for me!

It was the size of a large hound when I first laid eyes upon it, yet as I took the train away from Baltimore to Philadelphia, I saw it loping through the fields, twice the size of the passenger car itself. It needed not even run, just gently trotted along as each step carried it dozens of yards. Will it next reduce itself to the size of an ant, slipping through the crack under the door? I have blocked it with towels and sheets and done the same for the edges of the windows, but it pursues me without rest. Merely killing me is not enough for it, it toys with me as a cat with a mouse or a cruel child with an anthill.

Not five minutes before I barred myself in this hotel room did I feel a sharp pain on the back of my leg and glanced back to see the beast darting away through the legs of the throng of people, howling in delight as it did so. Blood trailed down the back of my calf, and there is a small piece of flesh no larger than my pinky nail missing. None heard it, of course. Neither did they see it.

The only other one who saw it was Neville, but he is dead, eaten by that horrible thing. And I am next. Neville was the one who encouraged me to go into the graverobbing business with him. There were a half-dozen medical schools in need of corpses, he told me, and each one paid quite well. Not to mention, it was rarely prosecuted, for there was no victim but ownerless, lifeless meat. He showed me a dozen articles in the paper of men who had been acquitted of grave robbery by a judge, despite them having been caught red-handed in the act.

Though I have no family to support nor children to feed, I do so love the finer things in life. Neville knew I would be happy to take the risk of digging up bodies in the earth for money. And indeed, I was. I was able to rent a room for cheap, which meant more for whiskey and women. I do believe Neville had a family though... God, will they even know he is dead? His corpse is almost entirely gone, and I watched in horror, knees frozen stiff, as his bones were crushed and splintered, his flesh ripped and torn.

Judges and prosecutors, Neville told me, turned a blind eye to the practice of corpse-digging, for doctors needed subjects to dissect and learn anatomy upon, and if the price of new men out there doing good in the world was for the corpses of a few to be dug up and desecrated, so be it. Together, we visited each of the cemeteries in and around the city—discovering which of them were frequently visited by the well-off and respectable, so we could avoid them. Or, if we were running short on funds, raid them. After all, Neville said in a whisper, slinging an arm around my shoulders, medical students quickly grew tired of the thin, bony wretches that were able to be easily grabbed from the potter's field where the bodies of the poor and dispossessed were dumped, and they would pay more for a refined corpse.

To me, it made no sense. Meat was meat, bone was bone; the spirit had fled up to Heaven with the Lord or snatched down to Hell with the Adversary, and their body left behind on earth like a discarded glove. But it didn't need to make sense to me; I just needed to understand it. And I did! *We* did! We didn't go to those cemeteries, keeping our deeds to the fields outside Baltimore where the dead with no family that cares about them are thrown.

But that's not enough, I suppose. Perhaps that thing fed there, and like a scavenger, we disturbed it? No, that isn't true. I see it in the eyes of the beast: intelligence and sadism. It knows what we are, what we do… and it hates us with the burning fury of the sun itself.

It was past midnight, and we were in the potter's field, loading corpses into our wagon. There's a trick to finding the good corpses, you see — ones where the flesh isn't too firm or too soft. So, it takes some time, and under the moonlight we managed to secure three corpses. A good haul, for though men die every day, it is never in such large amounts that there is a glut of corpses choking the graveyards. And good thing, too, for such places are breeding grounds for disease and decay, though we grave-robbers might have a brief period of more profits. We came to the end of the row, and began to make our way back the other way, when Neville exclaimed, bending down.

"Well, look here!" he cried, and held up to me a simple wooden charm. It was a wheel barely the size of my palm, with eight spokes spaced evenly within it. At the end of each of those spokes was a dangling feather, black as night and only visible by the white of their quills.

"Some pagan charm, I'd wager," I replied to him, patting the horses as I leaped from the wagon. "Let me?"

Neville nodded and handed it to me. It felt like a block of ice had been placed in my hand, and I yelped, tossing it back to him, as the other man caught it with a frown, resting the thing in his palm. "Lord, man, why didn't you mention the cold?"

"The cold?" he asked, looking at me. "What on earth do you—"

All in a single moment, that pagan charm changed. The eight feathers that hung from the edge of the wheel stuck directly out to the side, appearing like nothing so much as a waterwheel. Those spokes crumbled, falling away into a blackness speckled with stars. For a breath, Neville and I stood there, staring at what appeared to be a hole in the world. Then, the beast appeared.

A beak, large and grey, reached through, and with a single bite, chomped Neville's throat nearly in two. Gurgling, my business partner and a man who I considered a friend collapsed to the ground. His scarlet lifeblood splashed against the cold, hard earth, and ran down the hard beak of the beast. It pushed its way out of that wheel, expanding and unfolding as it did so, throwing its head back and gulping down Neville's severed flesh and howling in delight to the night air. The horses whinnied and panicked, galloping off and leaving me behind. I could not bring myself to move. I had never seen blood of that quantity before, never heard the tearing of meat and snapping of bone.

The hound-sized creature landed on the ground. It was feathered, with its dark plumage stained with blood. Its head was like that of a bird: beaked and with eyes on either side of its skull. Eight eyes, to be exact, each placed what seemed to be randomly on its cranium in utter defiance of natural law. It was if God's hand had simply poked holes wherever took His fancy, and left gaping orifices there, which had been filled with enormous eyes, yellow and serpentine, slit pupils twitching wildly. I swear on God Almighty, there was sadism and pleasure in its eyes! It knew it had slain a man and took such joyful pleasure in it I trembled to look.

It had eight legs—like that of a spider—and each ended in a foot with six talons, four facing forward and two facing back, each as long as a knife and twice as sharp as they cut into the muck of the earth. Cawing in glee and triumph, even as Neville choked, fingers pressing uselessly against his neck, the thing leaned forward and buried its beak in his arm, and I watched as it severed his forearm in the center. The splintering of bone, the ripping of the flesh... the thing threw back its head and swallowed it all, and I will forever remember the moment that I saw Neville's eyes glaze over and his eyelids flutter, his consciousness fleeing his flesh.

The cry of the beast was three parts caw of a crow to two parts howl of a dog. It pierced my ears with such a volume that I desperately threw my hands up to cover my ears, and I was certain the entire city of Baltimore heard it. Once more, it bent its head to the corpse of my friend. Finally, my knees unlocked, and I made to run away. Turning, I began to run—and fell. My boot caught on one of the corpses we had left on the ground. I tripped, sprawling across the earth.

Suddenly, the beast turned around. For a moment, all was silent but for the gurgles and twitches of Neville's failing body, and then the beast was in front of me, moving so swift and silent that I merely blinked and it appeared. The creature looked at me with those chaotic eyes, each scanning a different part of my body, as if looking for the slightest weakness. My breath came swift and my heart beat wildly in my ears—and then the beast smiled at me, cawed mockingly, and reached forward, taking a single nip of my nose. Blood, red and warm, trailed down my face and dripped onto my chest, and it spun around, scuttling back to Neville as it continued to feast upon his flesh.

I ran, then, and never looked back. My lungs demanded a respite, my legs screamed for mercy, but I did not stop running until I reached the President Street Station in the heart of the city, desperate to get away from that thing. But it followed me, through the crowds and down the train tracks, and now it scurries and scratches at the walls and doors of my hotel room.

I can hear it! *I can hear it!* Cawing and howling and laughing at me for daring to go to the fields of the dead, for taking something that was not ours to take. For when the spirit flees the body, the flesh of man stays upon the earth and is returned to it… It will give no quarter and desires none, for all it hungers for is the living flesh and pumping lifeblood of the living, after it has spent so long devouring the dead…

No! *No!* It shall not devour me as it did Neville. It shall not eat me piece by piece, savoring each bite of flesh while my soul still infuses the meat of my body with vitality! I will take the firearm I have ever kept in my luggage and send a bullet coursing through my skull; whatever that beast does with my body will happen only after. But I will not suffer it to torture me while I am still alive, for I swear in those eight eyes I saw the screaming face of Neville, twisted and howling in agony.

09

LOST IN THE DARK

My name is Daniel Marino. I am thirty-one years old. I was born in New York City on August 8th in the year 1893. I served in the Navy from 1912 to 1919 aboard the USS Des Moines as a Gunner's Mate First Class under Captain Smith, reporting to Chief Gunner's Mate Clark. The name of my mother is Mrs. Kathrine Marino. The name of my father is Mr. Samuel Marino…

My vision does not change whether my eyes are open or closed. It is pitch black, and I cannot remember how long it has been since I last saw even the faintest glimmer of light. There is no sound but for my own breathing and the shuffling of my clothing against itself, but even that feels like the naval guns are firing with how long it has been silent. The smell… it used to be horrific, I think, but my nose has long since adjusted, and if—no, *when*—I escape this place, it shall take months to return to normal. I have fallen asleep two times. No, three. Yes, it was three.

I cannot lose track of how many times I have fallen asleep. I'm certain of that. If I lose track of how many times I have fallen asleep, it will be the end of me. The first was hours after I wound up here. *Here* is… the tomb. The tomb in the Kingdom of Hejaz, yes, on the Arabian Peninsula. I went there after the war, hired as a guard for business interests. The Ottomans were partitioned and split, and that meant opportunity for the man who hired me. What was his name? He was British, I remember that much. Why can't I remember his name? I've only fallen asleep three times, haven't I? It started with a B… Bridges? Yes, Bridges.

Mr. Bridges was one of the many men who came to the Kingdom of Hejaz in an attempt to negotiate around the king. The king was no longer a fan of the British who had helped him gain his throne. Religious reasons, Mr. Bridges said, but there were nobility in the kingdom who were more than willing to sell the rights to the petroleum on their own personal lands—orders of their king be damned. They'd rather have foreign gold.

"Black gold is worth more, though," the businessman joked with me, nudging me as he snickered at the men who he had just been flattering with the most sincere smile on his face as he shook their hands and bowed to them.

They liked his money, but not the man himself. I agreed with those Arabian nobility. I smiled at Mr. Bridges jokes because he paid me, but the man himself wasn't very pleasant. Is that why I don't remember his name very well? Because I didn't like him? Yes, that would make sense, wouldn't it? Still, he was paying me well. Better than the Navy did by quite a margin, so I listened to him. *If a job is worth doing, it's worth doing properly*, my father said. Or my mother. Or—no, it was my uncle. I don't remember if he was my father's brother or my mother's, but I remember him saying it. And it *was* quite a lot of money.

He wanted to go into the desert. I advised him against it, there was only so much I could do to help protect him in a place like that, and nothing I could do if we ran out of water. Mr. Bridges dismissed all those concerns, though. He even offered me a bonus if we found... something. Yes, I remember now, he wanted to look for artifacts. Statues, vases, trinkets... he thought they would look pretty in his home. Or, failing that, wanted to sell them off to his other friends. The way he talked about it, he thought there would be Elgin Marbles over every dune, gilded masks of pharaohs buried in the sands, canopic jars lying against trees.

But we did find something. The tomb. I'm in it now, I think, though I can't remember properly. I remember being outside of it. I remember being inside of it. And I know that I'm here. So *here* has to be the tomb, doesn't it?

My name is Daniel Marino. I am thirty-one years old. I was born in New York City on August 8th in the year 1893. I served in the Navy from 1912 to 1919 aboard the USS Des Moines as a Gunner's Mate First Class under Captain Smith, reporting to the Chief Gunner's Mate... I don't quite remember his name. The name of my mother is Mrs. Kathrine Marino. The name of my father is Mr. Samuel Marino...

I've fallen asleep three times since I've been here, but I'm not yet hungry. I should be, shouldn't I? While I'm awake, I'm constantly moving, hand on the stone walls as I take step after step, trying to find my way out of this place, or at least find my way to a source of light. If I could see my hands again, even the faintest outline of them, I'd count myself a lucky man, but I've not seen so much as glimmers in ages.

Someone told me once—a school friend, I think—that if you just follow the left wall of a maze, you'll eventually find the exit. So, that's what I've been doing. But... I tripped once. Over my own feet, probably, or some tiny pebble or crack on the floor. I fell and felt my breath explode from my lungs, and it took me a moment to get back up and continue on my way. Is it possible that I placed my hand back on the wrong wall? Maybe. But it should be fine, shouldn't it be? I'll still go along every wall and line of that maze.

The tomb was like the Valley of Kings, carved into the side of the canyon with care and precision. Mr. Bridges insisted on going down there, so we did. I had no objections, but the local guide said something: the tombs were for the dead and the dead alone, that once the body was interred it was forbidden for any living soul to enter it. Stupid, senseless superstition. I didn't even bother telling Mr. Bridges about it, because I knew how men like him worked.

He may attend Sunday mass and place bank notes into the collection dish, but only so that he may be seen to be generous by those around him. The Arabic aristocrats were the same, but the guide… I saw the fear in his eyes. True fear. One that had been in my own eyes as the guns on the ship I served on fired, reflected back at me in the eyes of my fellow servicemen on… The ship I served on? It was… the USS… God, I can't remember! Why can't I remember? I was so proud of it, I rushed to tell my mother, my father, my cousins. The captain, he was Captain Smith, wasn't he? But that's such a common name.

Is my mind playing tricks on me? I can barely hear anything now, not even my own steps upon the floor.

My name is Daniel Marino. I am thirty-one years old. I was born in New York City in August in the year 1893. I served in the Navy for seven years aboard… aboard a ship. I was a Gunner's Mate First Class under Captain Smith, reporting to the Chief Gunner's Mate. The name of my mother is Mrs. Marino. The name of my father is Mr. Marino…

We went down to the tomb, yes, with Mr. Bridges behind me. The guide stayed up on the ridge. Is he still there? My employer promised him money if he did. But I've fallen asleep three times—or is it four? So, he's there no longer, almost certainly. If I get out of here, could I even make it out of the desert? The tomb wasn't that far away from the city, was it?

I entered the tomb first, and I still remember that first step clearly. I'm forgetting so much else, but I remember that step. It was like walking into a different world, stepping from the boiling, dry heat of the desert into the coolness and stillness of the tomb. I shivered from it, and sweat beaded on my brow with renewed vigor as my body tried to adjust to the new temperature. It was dead silent after I had stepped over the threshold, no sounds from the desert or from inside. And then Mr. Bridges charged over that threshold after me, complaining loudly about the heat and how glad he was to be out of it. I clapped my hands over my ears to protect my hearing.

We lit torches with a box of matches I had in my pocket—*the matches!* No, they're not in my pocket anymore. Did I drop them? Did I use them all up? I used a few in the beginning, after my torch died out, but if I had used them all, I would remember, wouldn't I? If I dropped them, I would remember, wouldn't I? Yet there's nothing in my mind regarding these matches, nothing at all. I walked in front, my employer behind. At first, I didn't think anything was wrong. It was just a tomb, like the ones I had seen in the textbooks about Ancient Egypt, and eventually we would come to the room where whatever ancient aristocrat had been buried. But we never did. Two minutes turned into three turned into five turned into ten, and we never found that room. My employer was furious, shouting about how every place like this had riches beyond compare placed next to their inhabitant's coffin.

I just let his words wash over me and kept walking, even as the man behind me huffed and puffed, his breathing slowly steadying from his fit of rage, fading into the background of my own breathing, my own steps, my own rustling of clothing. Then, I looked back, and he was gone. I shouted for him, and I heard no response. But maybe that's because I didn't call his name correctly… what was it, anyway? I backtracked and tried to find him, but I walked another ten minutes in that same direction, and I never reached the exit, and I never saw him. That's not possible, though, is it? There was no other path.

No other path… I've been following this wall for so long. I've fallen asleep… how many times now? A few, I think. Surely I'd have gotten to the exit by now? I couldn't possibly have been turned around every time, could I have?

My name is Daniel. I am thirty-one years old. I was born in New York City. I served in the Navy for… some time, a few years, perhaps. It was aboard… aboard a ship. What did I do there? The name of my mother is Mrs. Marino. The name of my father is Mr. Marino… That would make me a Marino too, wouldn't it?

Something's wrong. I'm forgetting things I shouldn't be forgetting. I used to know the names and ages of each of my cousins by heart, and now I can barely call them to mind. If I had cousins, I must have aunts and uncles, right? But I can't remember any of them now. I worked on a ship, but I can't remember who I worked under, or where. I must have worked on a ship in this area, right? That would explain why I'm here. Where is *here*?

A tomb, right, a tomb... that guide. He said that the tombs were for the dead alone. And the dead have no need of memory, or of light, or of sound, or of feeling...

My name is... what was my name? Surely, I had a name... once...

10
PARASITE

The first time I met a vampire, I was ten years old. Well, I call them vampires—I'm not sure what they call themselves. I've just made a habit of killing them wherever I find them.

I travel a fair bit for business, you see, and there's always one or two even in the smallest towns if you know where to look. It's a hobby, I suppose, as much as killing pests can be a hobby. Not pests, exactly. You know how as awful as mosquitoes are, they're necessary in a healthy ecosystem? I don't think the vampires are necessary to humanity's ecosystem, so they're less pests and more… weeds, perhaps? Yes, the idea of myself as a gardener of humanity is a pleasant one.

But back on track: I met a vampire when I was ten years old. It was the summer of 1979, in some city or town on the coast of California, and I was out playing with friends past sundown. I didn't really have a curfew and barely had parents to speak of — just two adults who lived in my home who made sure there was food in the fridge and occasionally woke me up by screaming at each other at the top of their lungs. So, I took any excuse to be out of the house for as long as possible. I was checking my wallet for cash — seeing if I had managed to scrounge up enough through mowing lawns and walking dogs to treat myself to a meal at one of the burger joints in town — when I heard a sound from behind me, and turned around to see a man looking at me from where he was sitting on a bench at a bus stop.

There was nothing particularly remarkable about this man, and that really is the thing you should keep in mind the most. Vampire novels and shows wax lyrical about their otherworldly beauty and grace, but that's an easy way to mark themselves out as being different from humans. No, they want to camouflage themselves among their prey. Real vampires look like ordinary people.

This one had blonde hair that came down to his shoulders, stubble, and was wearing beach shorts and a t-shirt. In other words, just one surfer among the thousands who inhabited the coastal cities of the state. Those are the types of communities they prefer, ones with itinerant members that can vanish and not return. These days, they tend to frequent the business class, those men and women who habitually live in hotels and barely stay at their legal address for a few days a month before having to leave once again. Oddly enough, I haven't yet found one disguising themselves among or preying upon the homeless. I'd wager that they don't taste quite as good as people getting regular, healthy meals, but I'm not going to ask them.

"Doing well, little man?" the vampire asked, arms spread wide and resting on the back of the bench.

"Yeah," I responded, closing my wallet and looking at him. I must have been clearly suspicious of him, because he laughed disarmingly, and raised his hands in the air.

"No need for that, yeah? Just makin' some conversation. Bus is always late, huh?"

"Yeah," I answered, relaxing a little as he made no move to get up from the bench. "Even the school buses around here are late."

"Well, that's a pain," he complained, letting his hands drop and lolling his head back. "I wanna get back to my place before midnight, at least. Too late to get back before sunset! But the waves were good, though, so who cares?"

"Dunno—never been surfing."

"Really?" The man was surprised, lifting his head and looking at me. "So close to the beach, that's a hell of a waste!"

"You think so?" I asked.

Here is the moment when he was able to get his hooks into me. The greatest trick of a vampire, you see, isn't transforming into a bat or mist, or being able to compel you with their voice. It's the fact that they have the skill to understand what makes you tick, to discover your deepest insecurities and fears and use them to manipulate you.

At this point, I've long since come to terms with the fact that I was an abused, neglected child. I had peers, yes, but there were never any people coming over to my house to play ball in the yard or to read comic books, and there was a fear in my heart of missing out on what my classmates and friends had. I saw how their parents treated them with love and affection and care, in stark contrast to how my own treated me, and I was jealous, scared of missing out on some vital experience due to their carelessness.

So, when he remarked that I was missing out on surfing—something which now, I am convinced was just him making casual conversation—he was able to tell exactly why I was shifting in place, why my gaze flicked away... and his perception of me changed from *camouflage* to *prey*.

"Tell you what," he said, leaning forward, "I'm not doing anything tomorrow. You wanna come down to the beach and use my board? Middle of the day, bright and crowded beach. No stranger danger, promise ya that!"

For a moment, I paused, wavering on whether to allow it. "What's your name?" I asked, and in that moment, he knew I was on the hook.

"Travis," he responded. "Your name, bud?"

"Ryan," I answered.

He grinned. "Nice to meet ya, little man. What say I see you down at the beach tomorrow?"

"Sure," I said, surprised I had agreed.

We arranged to meet at the beach, and though stranger danger had been drilled into my head from a young age… well, it was the summer, and it was in Southern California. To say there would be hundreds of people at the beach was an understatement to the extreme. So I went back to my house, and looked forward to tomorrow, eager to spend as much time away from my house as I possibly could.

I arrived at the beach at around 10 A.M., and Travis was already there, sitting on the short waist-high wall that separated the parking lot from the beach. Yes, vampires can be in the sun. If they suffer discomfort from it, I don't know, but of all the vampires I've found, the daytime has never been an obstacle for them.

He was dressed in swim trunks and a t-shirt—as was I—and grinned as I approached, bounding up and patting the board next to him.

"Heya, bud! Ready to learn how to surf?"

I nodded, an unconscious smile spreading across my face in response to his own.

He actually taught me how to surf, you know? I still remember how, and it's quite enjoyable on the rare occasions I'm able to take more than a day or two off. I'm not the young man I used to be, and I need some time to recover afterward.

I stayed far longer than I should have, and by the time the sun had set, we were still on the beach. Now, he had grabbed a volleyball from the back of his truck, and the two of us were hitting the ball back and forth. Again, you see the ability of the vampire to closely mimic exactly what its prey wants. I wanted an older brother, some figure halfway between a peer and a father, and he was able to provide something I didn't even know I wanted. I see it time and time again, now, though I can't blame their victims.

It's easy to rationalize something as "too good to be true" when it has to do with business or finances, but it is much harder to do so when that thing is emotional. It's what makes people overlook the red flags of their date or justify abusive behavior, all because some emotional need is being fulfilled.

Anyway, I don't want to dwell on it. On a certain level, it still hurts. I know that Travis saw me as prey. A disaffected youth who could be easily manipulated into being alone with a stranger and devoured, and it was only a combination of luck and adrenaline that saved my life. He was still the first adult to show any interest in me at all. Even though I know it was only a ruse, the human mind is a funny thing, to get attached so easily to things we know are lies. It was only a day that I spent with the vampire, but it was still enough.

The point is, he tried to kill and eat me. I was walking past the entrance to an alleyway, and suddenly my lungs were empty, my back hurt, and I was looking up at the cloudy night sky. Desperately, I struggled for air, disoriented as my eyes darted around and landed on the dark figure falling on me. Travis had tackled me down into the alleyway, and now he was on top of me, mouth wide open. He had no fangs. Instead, as I looked down his throat, I saw inside of it what could only be described as a worm. Past his tongue, rising from the darkness of his insides, was a long, white worm, with teeth like that of a leech, ringed in multiple circles around its own mouth. It was segmented, so pale I could see the veins pulsing beneath its skin.

This is a vampire. Not the human it holds as its host, but the parasitic worm inside that feeds on human blood. I have found them to usually measure between forty-four and fifty-six inches in length—though I've seen some stretch up to seventy inches—and are as thick around as one's forearm. It is a supernatural parasite. It strikes quickly, with the speed of a snake, but is otherwise fragile.

As I said, it was luck which saved me. I had no air in my lungs, dazed and confused. But as my hand closed around a chunk of concrete that had been placed to the side, I swung it toward my attacker, instinct having taken over my body and pushed me into the "fight" mode. The vampire inhabiting Travis lashed out at the exact same time, and in what was certainly the luckiest moment of my life, my wild, frantic blow struck the worm head on.

The screech was high and shrill, but quiet—barely loud enough to hear. The body of Travis collapsed and twitched and jerked on the ground of the alley next to me, having a seizure. I panted for breath, coughing as I tried to push air back into my lungs. My eyes darted over to the side, and I saw the pale worm likewise twisting and flopping on the ground, blood leaking from the wound I had given it when the jagged concrete slammed into its flesh.

Pushing myself up onto my knees, I lifted the concrete with both hands, and with as much strength as my small body could muster, brought it down with force onto the squirming creature. Once, twice, three times, over and over again until a good foot of the vampire was separated from the rest of its body. Gasping, I looked down at it, the long, pale thing itself having gone completely limp. Travis, on the other hand, was still shaking, though his motions were becoming less and less violent, his breathing becoming shallower.

I knelt there, unable to tear my eyes away, until he stopped moving and stopped breathing. Then, I heard a hiss, like water boiling, and I glanced to the side, watching as the flesh of the worm began to bubble, steaming away into the air. Staggering to my feet, I covered my mouth and nose with my scratched hands, and watched wide-eyed as inch by inch, that impossible creature dissolved into thin air.

That was the first time I saw a vampire. It was by no means the last. Like I said, I've killed many of them over the years. I've no evidence but photos and videos I took in the time before their corpses disappeared, and these days, so much can be faked on those fronts. So, dismiss me if you like, but just keep in mind how many people you've fallen out of contact with over the years, and ask yourself if you could find them again.

11
THE SCARLET WANT

Oft it is said to be wary of prophecy, for one often causes the outcome they seek to prevent.

Was it not Oedipus who, hearing of how he would slay his father and lay with his mother, never returned to his home, killed a man on the road, and married the queen of a far-off city? He was completely unaware that those who had raised him had never given birth to him but instead found him in a field and brought him up as their own out of the kindness of their hearts.

Did not Jesus, at the Last Supper, turn to Peter and say that the other man would deny him thrice before the cock crows?

Though Peter refused to believe it, he did so to preserve his own life, and was eventually forgiven by the Messiah after his resurrection.

When the father and mother of Siddhartha Gautama were told he would be a great king if he experienced no suffering or a great guru if he did, did they not ensure he wanted for nothing and knew no pain? And so, when he ventured outside the palace and saw the varieties of the human condition, it affected him so greatly that he sat under the bodhi tree for 49 days and 49 nights until he achieved enlightenment?

Such things are common in myth and in legend, in play and in story, and yet time and time again humanity goes forth arrogantly to prevent or sidestep the declarations of seers and proclamations of oracles—ignorant to the outcomes they will cause, thinking themselves the better of those in the past.

In the year of our Lord 1893, I was an occultist of the third rank in the Disciples of the Winter Sun. By this time, false occultism had become almost fashionable, and those fools and charlatans who merely played at magic and power like the Hermetic Order of the Golden Dawn provided such cover that when I told a friend I was heading to an occult meeting, the response was a jovial laugh instead of a shunning in proper society.

In those days, the man in charge was Andrew Alexander Lake, a barrister who funneled the payment from his law practice into the Disciples—who had been languishing in relative poverty for decades if not centuries. Occult practices and rituals are expensive, and he was made leader partially in acknowledgment that without his monies, the Disciples would have knowledge but not the means to implement it. This should not be taken to mean that he was a poor occultist. If anything, Lake was a somewhat talented one. But the truth is that he was perhaps the worst possible fit for the Disciples.

The Disciples of the Winter Sun are devoted to the occult principle of the cold and the dead, the silence and the eternal. NORTH is its name, and is likewise the direction the dead go. All those who surpass the first rank have been marked by it in some fashion. All of those, that is, except for Lake himself. It rankled him, I knew, to be the leader of a group and not be a part of it. When we sat in the stillest of silences, he would have to leave the room, for even the beating of his heart and the rushing of blood through his veins was too loud for the silence, too fast for the stillness.

He desired, he hungered, he wanted—more than anything else, how he wanted! And such desire is the occult principle of the Scarlet, which is so opposed to NORTH there are no words to describe the vast gulf of the distance between them. Yet if there had ever been a cult of the Scarlet in London, it would have long since disbanded. For all that Lake desperately desired to know that principle, he had not the ability to move to the Indian sub-continent where we believed a group of Scarlet devotees to be.

It was that desire, that want, that hunger, that led to his end. He suggested, one day in summer, that we advance our studies and perform a ritual more advanced than we had before. He suggested we summon an Oracle of the NORTH. He would provide, as always, all the money for the endeavor: hire those occult smiths needed to produce the mirrored pane of pure silver—exactly the length of the five spines of the five skeletons needed placed end to end—purchase and transport the ice from the North Pole, pay for the hogshead of animal blood needed to draw the Oracle back to the world... and all he desired was to ask a single question of five allotted upon summoning the Oracle.

How could we have said no? I was one of the nine at the third rank of the Disciples, according to the texts which had been passed down from the pagans of what was now Russia. My skin was always cool, and I could no longer drink hot tea lest it scald my throat, yet I had no idea how to take the next step. For to advance to the fourth rank, these texts said, one must take a step NORTH while still alive. This is, of course, not the same as taking a step north, for NORTH is the direction the dead go, and where such things as the Oracle are called from—a place so cold and still it will freeze the blood in the veins and the soul in the body. So cold it will leave one standing as a statue of ice forever in its domain, trapped, unable to return to wherever souls go. The nine of us needed to understand how to take a step there and return.

We agreed. Of course we did. And so, Lake spent money as if the end of the world was coming. Freely letting the artisans and smugglers and butchers drain his pounds as if they were in the desert, dying of thirst, and his cash was the life-saving water. And yet, how could we say anything when we would benefit? Regardless, he paid enough money. On the day of the winter solstice—that longest night of the year that all peoples and cultures understood in their bones had significance—we stood around the mirror. Lake watched from the other room nervously. In my pocket was a piece of paper with his question written. He could not be in the room with us, such was his opposition to NORTH, and we would be asking his question for him.

The five skeletons were placed at intervals of 72 degrees exactly upon the silver mirror, skulls touching at the exact center of the pane. Each of us stood at the feet of one of the bleached skeletons. The bones were white as snow as we began to chant, the balls of polar ice in the eye sockets of the skulls beginning to freeze over the rest of the skeleton. We all carried a barrel, filled with a fifth of a hogshead of animal blood, and together poured it over into the mouths of the skeletons. The warm liquid, steaming in the freezing air, spilled over the teeth and into the mouths, then vanished entirely from view. No longer were the skeletons made of bone, but rather of purest ice, clear and cold. As the last drop of blood disappeared, the skeletons stood up as one. Their eyes were portals to NORTH, I knew, and merely looking at them sent a shiver through my body.

Once, I stood nude in a blizzard all night. I thought I had surpassed the feeling of cold, and the Oracle made me feel like a child needing to bundle up once again. Those icy skulls were bound together, the backs melded as one, and their skeletal hands interlocked. Soon, there was no more movement, only silence.

Each of us was due a question, and we would advance in order: counterclockwise, from Christopher Smalls, who stood at the north skeleton, to myself, standing to his left. I had agreed to be the one to ask the question that Lake desired, and Christopher had agreed to ask that question the nine of us so desperately desired: how to go NORTH while still alive. The other three had likewise agreed to ask the last three questions we nine had agreed upon.

Of the answer the Oracle gave Christopher, I will not speak; let it be enough to say that the nine of us soon applied for menial jobs at the various hospitals in London soon afterward. The other three questions will likewise go unremarked. The rituals and workings we obtained from that Oracle still lie in the collection of occult papers and books of the Disciples.

When it came time for me to ask the question Lake had so desired, there was something that made me feel off... a sense of vertigo, as if I was on the precipice of a cliff and was about to fall. Gulping, I opened the paper with shaking fingers as the Oracle waited in the stillest of silences.

"How," I asked, "may the principles of NORTH and the Scarlet be married, to be balanced in a single man?"

I could barely believe my own ears, and neither could those around me. *How could they be married?* They could not be. Like ice and fire could not be married, for the ice would either extinguish the fire or be melted by it. It was a senseless question, and a waste. Yet the Oracle did not move, and the skull facing me opened its mouth.

"There is no balance to be found between NORTH and the Scarlet," it said in words of ice. "There is balance between day and night, yet not between NORTH and the Scarlet. There is balance between cold and heat, yet not between NORTH and the Scarlet. The path NORTH is not the same as the path to the Scarlet. A step down one is a step away from the other."

It said no more, the chill of the room fading from the stinging cold of a blizzard to the lukewarm of an overcast day, and I sighed in relief as the ice of the skeletons began to melt down onto the silver mirror. The five of us stepped back, smiling at each other, and would have laughed if not for those empty eye sockets demanding reverence. Together, we filed out of the room, leaving the skeletons to melt, the empty barrels on the ground, and closed the door behind us.

Lake was not pleased with the answer the Oracle had given him. I could not blame him. Before this, I had seen him as an arrogant fool, a man with more money than sense who threw his weight around, despite not being suited for the cult in which he found himself. Now I know better. That desire of his, that want, that thing which pushed him so deeply into the Scarlet that he was marked by it before he ever knew of the occult... it was merely to belong. So, I now see in him a tragedy, for with the words of the Oracle he had given up on the impossible act of balancing the two—yet not on retracing his path down the Scarlet.

"There are those who have embraced the Scarlet and die," he argued to me one day as we lounged in the sitting room, drinking cold tea—as was our habit. "It is only a lucky few who manage to go far enough along any path of an occult principle to achieve immortality. Before that, death is still something that plagues them all. Even those who have embraced the Scarlet. They step back from that and go NORTH."

He would not be persuaded otherwise. He journeyed to the foremost occult library in the United Kingdom: a mansion in Wales occupied by a devotee of the Radiance. He attempted to find something, anything, that could help him with his desire. Lake came back only with hints and extrapolations: stories of devotees of the Scarlet engaging in ritualistic cannibalism, who fed on the life in others to increase their blood such that it flew from them as if a fire hydrant had been broken; stories of disciples of NORTH that healed the sick by giving of their own blood to them, who were ice cold to the touch and bloodless, yet moved and spoke as if nothing was wrong.

Eventually, in the spring of 1894, he came to me. By this time, I had taken that step NORTH and survived—though my legal identity was dead of a stroke, my body having been unearthed by my fellow occultists. I now live permanently in the headquarters of the Disciples. I no longer needed sleep, I no longer needed food, and I no longer needed to breathe. I sat in my room, in utter silence and stillness, and contemplated NORTH. I shook Lake's hand when he entered, and he gasped as he did and pulled away. I saw small flecks of skin had frozen to my hand, leaving his own palm slightly bloody.

"I plan on taking the steps backward this winter solstice," he said to me. "Will you serve as my anchor point for NORTH? I just need to walk to you. Not too far, of course. It would be impossible for me to walk NORTH and live. But it should be enough for me to walk through the crossroads and out the other side."

"Do you think you know better than the Oracle?" I asked softly, and he blinked.

"I think no such thing!" he protested, indignant. "I am not trying to do something as absurd as marrying two opposing principles. I understand, now, how foolish that was—but just reversing a process. Surely that should be easy enough?"

"Is it easy to reverse the process of turning wood into charcoal?" I asked him.

"No," he admitted, "but I am neither wood nor coal."

I could not dissuade him. Perhaps I didn't particularly try. I am finding it harder and harder to care for things that are not heading NORTH. For all that Lake so desperately wanted to do so with us, the fact remains that his desire was so strong it tore him the opposite way.

The ritual Lake had designed was a failure, totally and utterly. I stood at one end of a courtyard while he began on the other. The goal, he said, was for each step he took to purge himself of the Scarlet and grow the influence of NORTH on his soul.

The first step went well, even as he bled from his eyes, nose and mouth. It was, he grunted, the influence of the Scarlet leaving his body. The desire and lust for life flowing out of him as he went NORTH, in the form of blood. Though those watching shifted nervously, he took another step, going pale as he did so.

He took one more step before he died. Lake froze there, in the dead center of the courtyard. Blood ran from all his facial orifices, freezing on his skin before running fast and hot again, then freezing once more. The Oracle spoke true: there can be no balance between the Scarlet and NORTH.

Lake had attempted to retrace his steps backward, but there is necessarily a center-point, midway between the principles of the Scarlet and NORTH. The moment he stepped there he was caught between the push of one and the pull of the other. I hope he died on the spot, but I don't believe that to be the case. After all, his body is still there, in the center of the inner courtyard. Every few moments, his blood goes from hot and steaming on his frozen skin to tracing his burning flesh with lines of ice.

No human has ever held opposing principles in equal balance. From the moment of our birth, we are affected by the forces both the natural and occult worlds alike exert on all things. I myself was born on a day in which multiple people died in the same hospital I was delivered at. Since then, I have held a slight inclination toward NORTH. Lake failed to realize that. Or perhaps he did, and merely convinced himself he knew better.

Either way, he is dead now. Just like those who went NORTH while alive, his soul is frozen in his corpse, even as the Scarlet within him attempts to keep him alive, pumping him with hot and boiling blood. He remains caught between the edge of two opposing forces, on the border of unreality. Forever, he is a lesson for other occultists.

142

12

UNKNOWN

The creature has been kept in our family forever as far back as our history reaches. From eldest son to eldest son, just as our family house is passed down through the generations, so too is the stewardship of that thing. That thing which has lived for centuries in the shed. It is human, or was once human—at least, I believe so—but is not recognizable as such even from a great distance.

Once, the family story goes, in the late 1800's, the caretaker took it into town out of some sense of pity or empathy for the thing. Yet he could not take it even a step into town before rocks started flying and men began yelling. Something about a leper, about the plague. The truth is, all who look on this poor creature know something about it simply is not right.

I remember the first time I saw it. It was the spring of 1946, and I recently returned from the fields of Germany where I had been deployed during the war. When I returned home, my mother wept openly along with my younger siblings. When they embraced me in a hug it took all my strength not to pull away. I returned it, as best I could, and told them how much I missed them. But when my littlest brother, Elijah, began to press me for stories from the war, my father stepped in and shooed them all away.

"Luke has just gotten back," he said, stepping forward and placing his hands on Elijah's shoulders as he gave a toothy grin. "Let him have his peace for a few days, will you? Now, have you finished your chores, or did you get too excited when you saw the car rattling up the way?"

Elijah's face fell, and a laugh forced its way out from between my lips as I stepped forward and ruffled his hair.

"I won't be leaving anytime soon," I reassured him. "There will be plenty of time later, okay?"

Nodding eagerly, he ran back into the house. My mother and sisters followed him with smiles and murmurs of how glad they were to have me back safe and sound, whole and uninjured. Then, it was myself and my father standing alone in the front, and he reached out his hand and shook mine, firm and steady.

"Welcome back, son," he murmured, and I simply nodded, unable to trust my voice. For a moment, we stood there together in silence, before he sighed. "Well," he said, "I'll give you a few days to settle in, Luke. Then…" Trailing off, my father stared not at me, but past me. Then he blinked, his eyes refocusing on me, and nodded. "Then," he said, seemingly having reaffirmed something to himself, "I'll have to show you your new responsibility, now that you're back."

That phrase consumed my mind for the next few days, even as I played with Elijah, read stories to my younger sisters, and helped my mother with whatever she needed. I settled back into the routine of home, one I had sorely missed after months on the front lines. Funny, that—if I ever told my little sister Sara I had missed life on the farm, I think she would have been utterly unable to comprehend it.

She was desperate to leave, always talking about how she was gonna go to the big city and be on her own, encouraged by Rosie the Riveter and our mother's efforts at the home front.

"But you left!" I could imagine her saying, eyes wide. "Why did you miss it?" How could I explain to her what war was like? The terror of the shells falling, how every crack of a rifle or thump of a mortar was a moment your heart stopped, afraid that it would never beat again. No, if I had my way, I would never leave this farm again.

After those few days my father had granted me, he placed his hand on my shoulder one morning at breakfast, and I knew it was time.

"Meet me in back," he said. I nodded, placing my plate in the sink, received a kiss on the cheek from my mother, and stepped out the back door. Usually, he smoked a cigarette, letting the smoke curl from his mouth like a smokestack from a factory, but he had none today.

"I don't smoke on days like this, where I have to take care of the responsibility," he said before gesturing to me. I followed him wordlessly, step after step through the fields, before my brow furrowed as I saw where we were headed.

"The woods?" I asked, almost murmuring the question, and he nodded. The woods were three or four acres of land on the farm that everyone was forbidden from entering.

Everyone has a tone of voice they use when they are absolutely not to be countermanded or crossed; the only time my father ever used his was when he told us that we were never, ever to enter those woods.

Together, we crossed under the canopy of trees, and as the shade covered us from the heat of the sun, I felt a chill slide up my spine. It didn't take very long for us to reach the destination. In fact, once I laid my eyes upon it, I wondered how I had never seen it before, through the trees. It was a building, smaller than a cabin but larger than a shed, made of wood and without no windows. From his pocket, my father pulled two things: a ring of keys and a flashlight. He handed the latter to me, and as I took it, he stepped up to the door of the building.

A glint caught my eye, and I sucked in a breath as I saw the number of locks on the door. There had to be at least half a dozen. I watched in confusion as he selected keys one by one, undoing locks with heavy clicks and thunks. Finally, he withdrew the keys, and sighed, placing them in his pocket.

"Go on, then," he said after a pregnant pause. "Turn on the light and head inside."

For a moment I hesitated before doing as he instructed. I turned on the flashlight, pointed it at the door, and taking a deep, long breath, walked inside. There were no windows or lamps inside the building, so the only lights that shone on the insides were the morning light that came through the door and the light in my hands.

I swept the flashlight over the bare walls, running it over old wood until it came to a bed placed in the far corner of the room, away from the door. I thought something had been tossed there carelessly, used as storage for a coat or firewood or one of the other countless things that a family generates over the years. And then I stifled a scream as two eyes opened in it.

It was roughly humanoid. It had a head, two arms, a body, and two legs, with no extraneous limbs or appendages. But even so, it could never be confused as human. No, it would look more at home in one of the freak shows of the last century, because there was surely no way something that thin should be able to move. Its own muscles should have snapped those thin bones in two. I could see the way they expanded and contracted, dark and translucent skin pulled taut over what remained of its emaciated flesh.

No more than five feet in height, its head was large and bulbous, oversized for its frame, and blue eyes like brilliant sapphires shone, wet and weeping, in its wrinkled face. Its skin was as dark as pitch—like leather left out in the sun for decades— but so thinly spread that I could see the bone white of its skull through its skin. A tattoo was spread across its face, but the ink was so faded all I could see was the occasional pencil thick line that suddenly vanished or reappeared.

The creature was oddly proportioned, with legs that seemed too short and arms that seemed too long, fingertips nearly brushing its knees as it stood up. Entirely naked, it seemed to have no genitals at all, and as it stared at me without blinking those strange, too bright eyes, I felt my breath catch in my throat. My paralysis was disturbed by my father's hand clapping on my shoulder. I staggered back, glancing at him, then back to the creature, as if it would make the sight before my eyes go away.

Stepping forward, my father got down to one knee and looked it up and down. "Are you alright?" he asked it, and I froze as I waited for that strange human-like thing to respond. It didn't, yet my father nodded anyways. "Do you need something?" he asked again, voice firm and clear as if talking to a child, and once again there was no response. A second nod came from my father, and he got to his feet.

"I will be back next week," he said, before turning and walking toward me. With a hand on my shoulder, he nodded at me, and I followed him out the door. Before it shut, I took another look back as it moved slowly to lay down on the bed again, stick-thin limbs trembling under its own weight, before the door closed and it was sealed away again. As my father locked the door behind us, he began to speak as I just stared out at the trees that surrounded us.

"For decades, from eldest son to eldest son, we've taken care of that creature on our land. The cabin was built some two hundred years ago, I think. There is little, if any writing that has to do with that creature, as I'm sure you understand now. How can you explain something like that if you've never seen it? As far as I understand, our ancestors took it with them when they left Europe for America, though I haven't any idea how they would have concealed it on the journey. Then again, it could likely just be put in a crate or something without issue. The cabin, as far as we know, doesn't even need to be there. We could probably just allow it to live outdoors and it would never stray, but such a thing... well, it seems to go against both human decency and Christian compassion.

"It needs neither food nor water, as far as I can tell, and just…
exists. It will stand when you arrive and stare at you, but I have
never heard it utter a sound, and neither did my own father or
his father before him, nor has it made any attempt to commu-
nicate through writing or pictures. As for what it is, or once was…
I haven't any idea.

"My great-great grandfather was convinced the creature was
once Cain, for he thought the faded tattoo on its head was that
mark God placed on him to prevent any man from harming him.
Yet he is no restless wanderer, so who knows? Who is there to
speak to about it? It simply is, and will continue to be, for as long
as the future continues.

"Now that you have returned, I will have you come and see
it every other week. Merely to check on it, though I don't
anticipate anything changing. It has not for as long as I or my
father have been its steward, and I anticipate the same being true
for you and your sons."

My father was wrong, of course, though I couldn't blame
him. He had never been to war, for he had a medical condition of
the heart that prevented him from the draft during the Great War.
He did not know what it was like to live on the front lines, that
constant sense of unease and panic that can take over your mind
and fill your thoughts and dreams with the terror of unknown
horrors just around the corner.

And so, I could not but think of that creature in the cabin. Cain, I called it to myself in an attempt to humanize it, to think of it as anything but that strangely proportioned thing that lived — no, not lived, but simply existed — on the farm where I had spent my entire life. It was as if the fear of foes I had spent so long keeping away, firing into the darkness of the night, was right there in front of me, and I was unable to do anything about it.

I encouraged Sara to follow her dreams, to go to the city and see what she could make of herself. In truth, it was less about caring about her and her dreams than wanting each of my siblings to be as far away from Cain as they could be. Every time I went to see it, my heart filled with dread and beat heavily in my chest, pulse pounding as I desperately tried to keep myself calm. Every time I walked in that room, even though nothing happened, it was like I was back on the battlefields of Germany once again.

When my father passed away some six years later, I wrote a letter to a friend of mine I had made in basic training. I had maintained correspondence with him for nearly a decade, and asked him to come visit me at my home. I had, I told him, important business to discuss in person. He worked for the FBI, at the time.

The important thing is that thing was gone from my land, and I could marry my love and move her into our farmhouse and sleep peacefully at night — never having to worry about that thing lurking in the cabin ever again.

Because far worse than the knowing that the enemy army was in the distance, able to blow a hole through your flesh if it ever left cover, is the *not* knowing, day after day, of if something one can't even call human might threaten those you love.

13
HATCHING MOON

It waits, high above us like the sword of Damocles! As the years go by, it begins to stir and wake, scratching at its shell with talons that will one day cleave through planets, pecking at it with a beak that will scavenge our world bare of life. Each crater, each imperfection, each canyon and mountain is a result of it twisting and turning, slowly growing until the day comes that it breaks out and renders humanity no more than a brief blip in the history of the cosmos; only a burst of radio signals that some alien species will receive as garbled background noise for a few decades before all goes silent again.

We must flee, if nothing else, for nothing we can do will kill it, and if it has not perished in the last uncountable eons that it has orbited our planet, it is almost certain we are not fortunate enough for it to die before it hatches from our moon and destroys us all.

My father was once an anthropologist, one who studied the cultures of the Pacific Islands. His grand work, as he once told me, was to create a solid timeline of the evolution of their mythology and belief system, from as far ago as he could manage. Something he knew was an impossible task but chased anyway with the passion and fervor of a much younger man.

Some of my fondest childhood memories are those in which he sat by my bedside, telling me all about the myths and legends of various tribes from the tens of thousands of tiny islands that dot that ocean like dust on a mantle. Each night, he would tell me a different story, of spirits and demigods, of tricksters and heroes, and I fell asleep to the bedtime stories of people a world away. It united me with them in that moment. Even though we existed under different stars and skies, across the equator and multiple continents, we still heard the same stories. We were still under the same moon.

I am fortunate my father was well respected and well paid for an anthropologist, and money was ever a distant concern for me. It led me early on to a passion for the arts. That I was able to attend college for it is a fortune I do not take likely. While I graduated without particularly distinguishing myself academically, I was able to do so artistically. Time and again, my professors praised me for my work, bold and striking and devoted to those folk tales and legends that my father had told me time and again.

My paintings were not the elegant, clean ones of the Renaissance era paintings devoted to the Greek and Roman gods and myths. No, my work was bold and jagged.

"Almost sketch-like," one professor said. I wanted to show how these cultures and myths were just as rich and historical as the ones every child in America or Europe grows up knowing. Indeed, there are more parallels than one might think. Well, in the end, my art is not important at all, except in that it is what let me know it is coming.

I dreamed of the moon for the first time a year ago now. I do not often remember my dreams, but in this case, it was so clear in my mind it hardly felt as if I had fallen asleep at all. I watched it the whole night, and it seemed as if I was watching a perfectly still viper. One coiled up, patiently watching me, waiting for its chance to strike out and puncture me with its fangs. When I woke up, I was struck with the sudden urge to paint that dream.

It was not, by my standards, a particularly remarkable painting. Merely a landscape of the moon, bright and large and steady over a landscape of trees that reached to the sky, framing it in what seemed like supplication. I placed it to the side and forgot about it entirely. It wasn't a commissioned work, just a moment of passion and artistic expression of a type I hadn't experienced in some years, and so I kept it as a reminder that I was still capable of joy when it came to art. When it came to commissioned works, while I still felt the satisfaction of a job well done, that youthful passion for painting had long since faded away.

I only remembered it when, two weeks later, I hosted a friend at my modest apartment. Adella Bergeron was her name, and though we once attempted a relationship, it had been our mutual agreement that we liked the other's company more as friends. Adella was from Louisiana, a lovely young Cajun woman. She was such a firm believer in the superstitions and folklore of her grandmother that she now made a living as a fortune-teller, attended to by the skeptics who wanted a thrill and the believers who were desperate for advice alike.

That night, our conversation drifted to and fro, as it so often did, and when I got up to refill our drinks, I found her staring at the painting I had made of the moon those weeks ago.

"When did you paint this, Matthew?" she asked, voice low and steady.

"A few weeks ago," I told her, shrugging. "I dreamed of the moon and was struck with inspiration. It looks quite lovely, doesn't it? The trees almost like worshipers, bending to their god—"

"It was the night of the fifth, wasn't it?" she cut me off, and my mouth closed. There was silence for a moment before Adella slowly nodded. "I dreamed of the moon that night as well. In my heart, there was such a terrible dread that I could hardly bear to breathe, lest something notice me. It may have been the strongest premonition I have ever experienced… I must go, I think. I have to speak with a friend of mine to see if they dreamed of the moon as well. Can you speak with your other friends? Ask if they dreamed of the moon, that night. I think they may have, and if that's true…"

Adella's voice trailed off, and she shook her head. Her brow furrowed, and she looked near ready to cry. I stepped forward and attempted to pull her into a comforting embrace, but she took a step back, attempting to return a smile instead.

"I'm sorry, Matthew. I will be seeing you soon, I promise." Reaching out, she took my hand and held it for a long moment, before squeezing it tightly and dropping it, leaving my apartment.

It was not yet three in the afternoon, and so as I watched her go—a dear friend of mine clearly panicked and scared at the coincidence of us sharing dreams—I resolved to help allay her fears by speaking with my friends, as she had requested. But of course, there was nothing that could be done to help her. After all, as I went about the city, speaking with each of my friends— artists, writers, poets—one and all, they agreed with me. They had also dreamed of that moon, bright and full, shining over landscapes that seemed to bow in reverence.

For some time, I thought about lying to Adella about it. Telling her that no other friends of mine had dreamed of the moon, that everything was fine… but I couldn't, not when I remembered her face so clearly distraught and upset. When she came to me, having herself spoken to the bohemians and the spiritually inclined of the city, I told her the truth of just how many had seen the moon, silent and still, and thought it watching them.

Adella sat in my living room, silently, holding her head in her hands. I tried to give her a glass of water, and when she refused to take it, a flask of the whiskey we shared so often. She simply shook her head and leaned back, tears in her eyes.

"They all dreamed of the moon," she spoke, almost choking up. "Each and every one of them."

"I've dreamed of it again since," I said, taking a seat next to her on the couch, and cautiously reaching out, placing a hand on her shoulder. "The moon began to stretch and deform, as if it were a blanket surrounding some creature inside."

Nodding, she leaned her head against my shoulder. "That is what my friends have confided in me," Adella whispered, tears beginning to fall. "Oh, to think it will come in our lifetimes…"

"What?" I asked her.

"The end of the world," she answered, and refused to speak any more that night, merely kissing me and bringing me to bed. When I woke up in the middle of the night, she was gone, though she had locked the door behind her and left a note apologizing for her absence. I was concerned for her, of course. This was all out of character for her, so I visited her apartment after a few days of polite waiting to allow her to collect herself.

Only after some minutes did she open the door, dressed in a bathrobe, with eyes puffy and hair tangled. With a choked sob, she embraced me as I stepped inside, clinging onto me as tightly as she could. Her apartment was laden with candles and paintings and statuettes, and the smoke filled my nose as I held on to her, trying to comfort her as best I could.

"Have your dreams changed?" Adella asked me, voice hoarse.

"Yes," I admitted, for I knew that if they had changed for me, they had changed for her as well. "Now, I see the shadow of the beast inside the moon, as if a great light has been placed behind it—one so powerful it illuminates through its shell. It twists and turns in its slumber, for it has yet to be born, and when it does, it will break the moon in half, destroying our world by accident through the destruction rained down onto us, and by purpose, for it will hunger when it is born."

"I cannot even blame it," she whispered, "for it is nothing but a beast. One might as well blame the chicken for devouring bugs on the ground. It is mere instinct, and nothing more. The disposition of its organs, as Descartes once said. There is no form of higher reasoning, no better nature we can appeal to. Can a worm appeal to a bird? There is some small comfort in that, at least."

"Can we flee?" I offered shakily. "Once, the newspapers said it would take millions of years for us to create a machine capable of flight, and yet now airplanes fly daily…"

"Flee to where?" Adella asked. "To space, that infinite void beyond the atmosphere of our planet? How could we ever do such a thing? For we need air to breathe, food to eat, and water to drink. By necessity all these things will eventually disappear, even if we could craft such a ship to take us far away from here. No," she concluded sadly, "it is the fate of humanity to perish alongside our Mother Earth."

I shook my head, pulling her tighter into my arms. "There must be some way," I said, but I knew even as the words left my mouth that it was a feeble protestation. God, what can we do? What do we even have the options to do?

Truthfully, there is nothing we can do but languish, now, for though the bohemians of the world are the ones who have these dreams, who know the warnings for that great shape that even now begins to stir, we have neither the knowledge nor ability to escape this planet we are so inextricably bound to.

I have, on multiple occasions, attempted to speak with those more intelligent in the matters of the sciences, but each and every occasion have I been rebuffed and sent away with scoffs and disparaging remarks about "dreams." Dreams they may be, but dreams have long been considered portents of what is to come for a reason. And now, I think we may not get the chance to dream much longer.

It will not be long before whatever creature rests inside the moon to hatch. And so, Adella and I will languish here, alternating between despair and impotent fury, until we finally find the will to take our own lives before we are devoured.

162

14

THE ASSISTANT

I only did it because she was threatening me! You have to believe me. You had your guys run the tests, right? You saw what she did to me! I had no choice, otherwise she would kill me—worse than kill me! I can feel it, constantly, her fingers tracing across it every now and then; a gentle squeeze to remind me she's in control of me. She has my heart, and she said she'd do so much worse if I said no.

You know how everyone says "Oh, he was such a quiet and respectful man, kept to himself, had no idea he could do something like that" whenever someone gets caught as a serial killer or cannibal or necrophiliac or something?

Everyone knew Amy was a freak from the moment they met her. It's not our fault; she's just creepy! She doesn't look at you right. Most people, their eyes move, they light up, they recognize you. Amy just looked at you like you're a signpost. I swear to God, she showed more emotion looking at an ant colony that she does looking at another person.

I went to primary with her, and she was like that even as a kid. Constantly reading weird stuff, asking stupid questions, completely ignoring me when I tried to talk to her… Yeah, so I messed with her a little. It was playground nonsense—it meant nothing! Everyone was doing it. So why did she go for me? I barely even did anything. Pulled her hair, dumped some water over her head—kiddy stuff, the type of thing girls do to each other all the time.

I wasn't even involved with her in secondary. We went to the same school, sure. We had to, given that we lived only a few blocks away from each other. A whole different group of girls were the ones messing with her then. I had way better things to do. I had band practice, and a boyfriend, and friends, and I didn't have any attention to give to some creepy girl that I barely remembered the name of but to tell someone, "Yeah, I went to primary with Amy, she's always been a freak!"

Olivia was the girl going after her in secondary school. She said that Amy stole her boyfriend, but that's a bullshit excuse. No one who ever met Amy for a second would believe that. That girl had as much interest in boys as a corpse. Maybe she was into girls, but I'd sooner believe she has no idea what sex or romance is. So Olivia probably was just finding a good time with it. And it's not like she ever said anything about it. Amy never told a teacher or anything, so who cares? Everyone knew it was happening, and no one said anything about it either! Olivia was the one who came up with all the bad stuff, the stuff that went from schoolyard teasing to actual harassment.

But who cares? Stuff like that happens all the time, and from far worse people than Olivia. Besides, Olivia was great. Top of her classes, popular, on the girls' football team as the striker. If she decided to pour soda into Amy's bag once or twice, who'd care? Sure, it got way worse once Amy and Olivia ended up in the same A-level classes and Amy started getting higher grades. It's understandable, though, right? Olivia worked her ass off, and there Amy was just walking into class with perfect scores and acing her tests in a half-hour or less.

Who am I fooling? Olivia was just going after Amy because she could, and I didn't say anything because I didn't care. Olivia was my friend, and Amy was that weird creep nobody talked to, and no one cared when she got harassed because no one cared about her. But she still should have gone after Olivia! I didn't participate, I didn't tell a teacher, I minded my own business, and this is what I got for it!

But apparently that weirdo held a grudge. I completely forgot about her. She went to a university overseas and I went to a university here, and she slipped my mind entirely. I had a new boyfriend, new friends, and a life, while apparently Amy figured out how to do… whatever it is she did.

I didn't even know she was back in town. My mum mentioned it, said that she had graduated early by taking more credits than she needed each year. She talks to Amy's parents now and then, I guess, at the supermarket or the community center or wherever it is that parents meet to talk about their kids. "Good for her, I guess," that was the extent of what I was thinking. Again, I didn't remember her. I didn't think anything of her! But apparently, she remembered me.

I don't know how she found me. Stalked me when I was going back from my mum's house, I reckon, little freak that she is, then just… waited, I guess. No idea how she got into my flat, let alone into my room without setting off the alarms. I woke up to her sitting on my stomach, looking down on me. The curtains were up, and I could see her face clearly in the moonlight. Her long black hair fell around her face like she was one of those creepy ghosts, and there was a small little smile on her face. I tried to scream. Obviously, I tried to scream, but nothing came out. My vocal cords wouldn't move. I could open and close my mouth, I could breathe and swallow and all those things that a human needs to function, but I couldn't speak. I couldn't move, either. I was frozen to where I was on my bed, unable to thrash or squirm. All I could do was lay there under her, paralyzed in place. I've heard of sleep paralysis but never suffered from it. That must be what it's like, to be forced to stay in one place as something terrifying looms over you.

"Hi, Julie," Amy said, and my gaze snapped to her. She was smiling down at me, and reached out, patting me on the cheek with one of her hands. "It's been some time, hasn't it? I wanted to come and show you some of the things I've learned while I was overseas. I need some help, after all, and after how you used to treat me... I think you're going to be my perfect assistant. Here, let's just..."

She took her right hand and reached down. Into me. The tip of her finger touched my breast and went through. It makes me feel nauseous and sick just thinking about it. Amy's hand moved through my flesh like it was water, my skin rising around her wrist like she had stuck it in a bucket and the water level was rising. I can't describe the feeling. There's nothing to compare it to—no point of reference. I've been cut before by a kitchen knife, but this wasn't anything like that. There was no pain, just a feeling of mild discomfort, like I was being lightly tapped. In my mind, I was shrieking and howling in confusion and terror, but I was still laying there, unable to do anything but watch as her hand passed through my flesh and through the bones of my ribs.

I felt her fingers against my heart. I've had heartburn before, once or twice, in those early years of college when I was eating unhealthily. It was like that, but not like it at all. There was a hand wrapped around my heart, four fingers and a thumb lightly resting against *my heart*.

And then Amy pulled her hand out, taking my heart with her. In trembling, quivering fear, I watched as my heart left my chest and continued to beat in the palm of her hand. The apertures where veins and arteries would be attached were perfectly cut and smooth, and blood didn't spill at all, still pumping into one part of my heart and out through the other, even though it wasn't in my chest anymore. I might have passed out, then, if I could, but I think that before she woke me up, Amy made sure I couldn't. I think she wanted me to watch the entire thing, for some sick kicks.

"It's great, isn't it?" Amy asked, even though I could barely hear her over the rushing of blood in my ears and my own thoughts. "A neat party trick for sure, but there's a lot more I can learn, I think."

Gently, she began to squeeze, and I could feel it, as those fingers dug into the muscle of my heart and the red meat bulged between her fingers. My back arched in pain, and I couldn't make a sound, even though I wanted to scream my throat raw. Amy relaxed her fingers, letting my heart rest in the palm of her hand, and smiled down at me, reaching with her other hand and stroking my heart like it was some kind of animal.

"So, you get the idea. Say anything, this goes pop. Do any-thing other than what I say, this goes pop. If you don't answer me when I ask, this goes pop. My number is already in your phone. I'll see you tomorrow, Julie."

And then she left. Just walked out of my room, heart still in her hand, and I saw her slip it into her pocket as she went. I swear to you, I could feel the denim of her jean pockets on my heart. I lay there, frozen, for what felt like hours. It *was* hours, actually. By the time I was able to sit up again, the sun was shining in through the window and I had to grab my phone and call off work on account of feeling like I was going to vomit my guts out. Which I did.

I didn't do anything. Obviously, I didn't. Amy had just taken my heart from my chest. Who would believe that? And if I did tell anyone, I could feel my heart. Could feel how every once in a while, a finger would trail across it, slowly tapping it. I knew Amy had it, but I didn't know if she could... I don't know, see where it used to be? Hear things from me? Nothing was too insane, no paranoid idea too much. She had just taken my heart.

My phone dinged as I was leaning there, over the toilet, and I looked at it with bleary eyes. It was a text from her, of course. She had put herself into my phone. Just her name, and a heart next to it. Sick girl. The text just had an address of a coffee shop nearby, and a time. "See you soon!" it read. What other choice did I have? I got to my feet and got ready to go out. I took a shower, threw on some clothes, and left. Usually, it would take me much longer to get ready, but for obvious reasons, I didn't particularly care about making sure my outfit was perfectly coordinated that day.

I arrived at the coffee shop, and I must have looked like crap, because I got a few stares. Amy looked just as creepy as she had in secondary—all dressed in dark colors and heavy layers, sitting at a table drinking a coffee as I got there. I didn't bother greeting her, just stood there and waited for her to acknowledge me, which she did with about as much remorse as a kid who'd just stepped on an ant.

"Great to see you again, Julie," Amy said, smiling up at me. "Let's get a coffee, and maybe a muffin, hmm? Then we'll head down to the park and have a chat."

"What do you want?" I bit out. I'd like to say that I was defiant, but in truth I was bloody terrified. Whatever magic she did was still playing in my head on repeat, and the idea of her just reaching into her pocket and crushing my heart was occupying my mind almost entirely.

"I'm thinking… chocolate chip for the muffin," she said. I genuinely wanted to hit her, damn the consequences. "How about you?"

"You know what I meant," I hissed, and instantly regretted it as she turned to me, that same smile still on her face. A hand slipped into her jacket pocket, and I tensed as I felt it, those five fingers wrapping around my heart. Amy put just the tiniest amount of pressure on it, like pushing down a key on a keyboard.

"Let's have that chat at the park, shall we?" she said, and it wasn't a question in the slightest. "I've changed my mind. Banana nut muffin for me, I think!"

She waited patiently for her muffin. Stood in line like nothing was wrong and bought another coffee. She stood back and looked at me expectantly, that small smile almost accusing. After a few moments, I stepped in line and ordered a coffee with some milk and sugar, as well as a chocolate chip muffin. It doesn't really matter, I guess, but it's still stuck in my mind. Amy was so insistent on everything being normal, like we were just two friends going for a regular meetup. I'm sure I don't need to tell you that I wasn't able to drink much of my coffee or eat much of my muffin. Just a bite and a sip, really, while Amy happily chowed down.

We walked down to the park barely two blocks away in silence, and once we arrived, Amy sat down on a bench and finished off her muffin with glee as I waited in front of her in silence. Letting out a sigh of contentment, she tossed the wrapper in a garbage can and looked up at me.

"So, remember what I said last night?"

I gulped. "Yes," I murmured, playing with my fingers. "Do what you say or…"

"Or your heart goes *pop!*" Amy beamed, leaning back on the bench and spreading her arms across the back. "I'm glad you remembered, I was worried for a second! I'd hate to have to kill you already. You haven't even helped me with anything yet."

"What… what do you want me to help you with?" I asked.

"Simple," she said, patting the bench next to her. I sat down, biting my lip as she continued. "I need more people to practice with. So, you're going to be my assistant, and help me get some."

What I felt in that moment wasn't fear or terror—it was just confusion. I was confused about what she was saying, like her words had gone in one ear and out the other, without making a stop at my brain in between. "Get people?"

"Exactly!" Amy answered, smiling at me. "Not too hard, is it? I don't care if you get some guy back to your apartment by pretending you'll have sex with him, or if it's a friend you say you just want to hang out with. You bring people back to my apartment every… let's say Saturday night. Otherwise…"

And then she slipped her hand into her pocket and started to squeeze, and I gasped out loud, doubling over as the pain in my chest intensified and shot upward. Sweat began to bead on my brow, and I groaned in agony as she continued to grab onto my heart. "If I could get an 'Of course, Amy?'"

"Of course, Amy," I gasped, and immediately the pain stopped.

"See, that wasn't so hard, was it?" Amy asked, reaching over and patting my shoulder. "I'll see you Saturday, then! Any questions?"

"No, Amy," I said. What else could I say? She was nuts. I couldn't do anything against her. I couldn't say no or otherwise she'd have murdered me. Crushed my heart and let me die, then push my heart back inside of me and made it look like nothing was wrong. You understand, right? There's gotta be some sort of law about this, isn't there? If you're forced to do something? There's a gun to my head—my heart—and it's still there. She still has it. I can't feel her fingers, but if she gets to wherever she's keeping my heart, all she has to do is squeeze. You have to find Amy. Please.

I did what she asked. That first night, it was just some random stranger. I went dancing and brought him back to the address that Amy gave me. It was like someone else was piloting my body, and I was just sitting in the back, waiting, watching as I flirted and laughed and danced. Julian. That was his name. He was about my height, if a little shorter. His laugh was sweet, and his grin was infectious. We joked about how similar our names were.

We walked back to the flat Amy had told me about, and though we kept laughing and talking, I couldn't feel anything. I couldn't feel my feet impacting the ground, I couldn't feel the coolness of the night air, couldn't feel the way his arm wrapped around my waist. All I could feel was Amy's fingers stroking my heart. I took out the keys Amy had given me and opened the door, and when I saw her sitting on the couch reading a book I almost screamed.

She introduced herself as my roommate. Julian apologized for interrupting her evening and offered to take me somewhere else. Amy shook her head and said that I'd asked her to leave, and she was just enjoying the last few minutes before I got to have some fun. My ears were filled with white noise, barely able to hear anything outside my own heartbeat; and I felt like my knees would buckle at any moment as she placed the book on the coffee table, then stood up and walked to the door. It was almost in slow motion that I saw her hand reach out and touch Julian's neck. Immediately, he dropped to the floor, entirely limp, like every muscle in his body had stopped working at once. I wanted to do the exact same, even as Amy smiled at me.

"Follow me," she ordered, and I mindlessly obeyed. I followed her, walking behind her as she guided Julian into the back room, where a second bedroom would normally be. It was painted white, and in the middle were two identical white tables, like a child's nightmare of an operating room. She stripped Julian, leaving him in just his boxers before placing him on one of the tables. I wanted to say something, but the words stuck in my throat like a bone.

She hummed, reached into her pocket and pulled out her phone, then pressed a button. Jazz, low and soft, started drifting through the room, and for the first time I noticed a speaker that had been placed in the corner of the room. "Just to keep things fun!" Amy explained to me, winking, before turning back to Julian and reaching inside of him. The first thing she did was pull out his heart, placing it on the small table as it beat steadily. She made me stand there and watch as she disassembled him, piece by piece. Organs first, placing them on that second table like a messed up, still-living anatomy diagram. Then the bones, one by one, all two hundred and six of them until he was a breathing pile of meat—no structure or form because Amy had taken everything out.

After she had taken Julian apart, she turned to me and smiled. Her hands were completely clean as she walked up to me and patted me on the cheek. "Thank you, Julie," she said, then kissed me on the cheek. "See you next week, sweetie. Bye!"

I left. I didn't want to be in her presence for a moment longer than I needed to. I try not to be, and she doesn't seem to care what I do so long as I show up each Saturday night with a new person at her flat. She makes me stay and watch as she takes them apart and afterward sends me off. Twenty-one weeks, I've done that for her. Which means twenty-one *people*.

Amy's a psycho. She's insane. I don't know how anyone could do that and smile like she does. A power like that... it could be used to help people, couldn't it? But she just wants to experiment, like a kid mixing dirt and leaves and water and juice, then calling it a magic potion. There's no rhyme or reason, just random ideas that pop into her head and that she decides to act on.

She occasionally tells me she's had a great idea, then shows me something. That's what *you* found, right? What led you to that flat. One of those messed up creatures she made for kicks, escaping out a window or something? Amy's made a whole lot more than just the one. It's like building blocks to her, stuff to take apart and reassemble as she pleases. I don't think she sees people as real—just raw material, flesh and organs and bones. There's no other explanation for what she does or why she makes things like that.

There was one she made that was like a spider, but with eight arms sticking out from the sides of that lump of flesh that was its body, each with eight fingers. She thought it was funny. It had two faces, one in the front and one in the back, each with eyes to see and a mouth to breathe and eat. I vomited, then, and she just sighed in disappointment and told me to mop it up, so I did.

Amy... she's crazy. I don't know how else to put it. She doesn't think like a normal person; she's something else. I don't even know if she can classify as a person anymore, with how she's treating everyone like a new bag of toys to take apart and reassemble. I'm sorry, I'm rambling. I'm just—I'm tired and scared and I've been living in hell for the past five months. I know what I did was wrong. But there are laws about it, right? There have to be, if someone puts a gun to your head and makes you commit a crime. That's what happened to me. You know it. You've seen the x-ray, how there's an empty space where my heart is. She has it. She still has it, and she's going to squeeze and pop it any minute now, I just know it…

Can I have some water? Please?

*

Julie Donovan's statement was paused so that an officer could fetch water while the attending detective remained in place to observe. Shortly afterward, she began to convulse and fell over. She had no pulse, and though attempts at CPR were made, with no heart in her chest, it was impossible to restart her circulation or breathing.

She was pronounced dead at 5:13 P.M. on August 12th, 2006. In regard to the forty-nine missing persons cases that have been connected to Amelia Finch so far, Julie Donovan was seen with twenty-one of them. It is therefore likely Amelia Finch possesses other accomplices, whether they are helping her willingly or are being forced to cooperate.

On August 14th, at 2:04 A.M., Julie Donovan's cadaver was stolen from the morgue. Security footage shows a man roughly eight feet tall with four arms breaking in through a window, then battering down the door to the morgue and taking her corpse before leaving the way he entered. It appears this man (referred to henceforth as Patient One) is a creation of Amelia Finch.

The following note was left by him in the body rack in which Julie Donovan's corpse was being kept:

Sorry, but Julie is mine. I'll make sure she comes back to finish her statement, though. Just you wait!

The handwriting on the note is identical to samples retrieved from letters and postcards addressed to Amelia Finch's parents from Amelia Finch herself.

15

RIVER THING

There are things in the river. I know it to be true, even if the police have only stopped short of saying that they think my little brother is crazy. They're not aware I know they're liars, of course, and for many other older sisters, a firm statement from the police would have been the end of things. David is many things, but that terror in his eyes when he told me something pulled Jimmy into the river was real, and I believe him completely. I saw it myself, after all.

Jimmy was my brother's age, about eleven years old, and he was the town daredevil. By the time he was ten, he must have broken his arm three times climbing trees or riding his bike or in some other hare-brained stunt. He was a likable kid, though, always grinning, always playful, yet still able to be properly respectful at school and church. Sure, people kept on trying to tell him he needed to be careful, that doing stunts like that was dangerous—but in the end, he always came out the other side beaming, even if a little bruised. Unfortunately, as parents every-where have learned, it only takes a single time when a child isn't lucky to turn a life into a tragedy.

David came running into town, soaking wet and clothes torn, screaming for help at the top of his lungs. Mr. Grady was the first person to see him. When he called out, David made a beeline for the older man. He was babbling and panicking, barely able to get out that Jimmy was in the river, and someone had grabbed him. Mr. Grady was the owner of the one convenience store in town and was a veteran of the Korean War. Thankfully, he wasted no time sprinting toward the river to try to find Jimmy, telling my brother to find the few members of our town's fire department.

Once David got there, they called the house right away. Both our parents were out, so I took the call. I sprinted down to the station, worried and scared sick. And so was David. I had never seen him so scared, so terrified. I saw it in his eyes, in the way his body shivered into me was I hugged him. Whatever had hap-pened down by the river with him and Jimmy, there was no denying it had shaken him to the core.

The rest of that day is a blur to me, quite frankly. I remember the arrival of Jimmy's parents and older brother, eyes wide with panic and fear. Deep down, I think they already knew the truth: one of his stunts had finally caught up to him, and they would never see their son again. I remember they found his shoe, a scrap of his shirt. I remember the low, keening noise from his mother, so utterly filled with anguish and despair.

Jimmy was never found, of course. David said, repeatedly, that something had leaped out from the water and grabbed Jimmy, pulling him down into the water. No one believed him; they just thought it was the overactive imagination of the child who had seen something traumatic. Those few who believed him thought there was a more innocuous explanation. That a fish had leaped from the water, startled Jimmy, and caused him to fall. No, there was something else here. Something that truly terrified him, something beyond the mere imagination of a child.

That night, I left the house as silently as possible, slipped through the door, and put on my boots before making my way down to the river. My breath misted in the cold air. I rubbed my hands together as I tried to rationalize away my desire to come and see for myself. But in my heart, I knew it was simple: I believed my brother more than I did the police.

It was pitch dark by the time I got to the river. As I crept forward, my heart began to beat faster, my spine began to tingle, and my breath came in short gasps. Something was wrong. I could feel it *in my bones*. Once, the biology teacher had described that part of the symptoms of a heart attack or a stroke was a "sense of impending doom." I felt that now. It was like there was something over my head about to fall, like I was sitting in the gaze of a predator I couldn't understand.

The moon shone bright and clear alongside the stars as I crept to the bank of the river, staring at the dark running water. Reaching out, I gently brushed my finger into the cold water, the icy feeling slicing through my flesh and to my bones. Slowly, I withdrew it, before standing up and walking forward. I paced along the bank of the river, driven by something I had yet to see, desperate to get a glimpse of whatever my brother had seen that had driven him so fearfully away. And I got my wish.

It began with a small bubbling in the center of the river, something that drew my eye for a moment. It kept my attention as the bubbles began to grow, as the water began to rise and cascade down the back of that thing that my brother had seen. My hands flew over my mouth, and I dropped to my knees, hiding as best I could behind a tree as I watched it emerge from the water.

I can think of no proper animal to compare it to. If I had to, I would name it some type of toad or frog, short and squat, but nearly twice the size of a horse, if not even larger. Innumerable eyes—too many to count—blinked out of sync with each other. The paleness of its throat swelled and contracted like that of a frog's croak. Over its whole body, it was mottled with browns and greens and deep reds, like the ground in fall, and its tongue lolled from its mouth like a hound's, though it was exactly like that of a toads. Eight legs jutted from its body at odd angles, with toes at perfect intervals on the base of the foot.

Those legs then began to move, steadily plodding along the riverbed, disturbing the water as it went. I watched it go—and possessed by some mad instinct, began to tail it. On my hands and knees, I crept behind it. Any sound made by my body cracking twigs or shifting stones was entirely drowned out by the sloshing and burbling of the water, of the croaking and gulping of the beast that was making its way through the river. The creature that devoured Jimmy.

I crawled after the beast through the riverbanks and tried to keep my breathing low and steady. I feared that at any moment— like the frogs I had seen by the pond in my youth—its massive tongue would lash out and wrap around my waist, pulling me into that maw and into the ranks of the men and woman who vanished. How many creatures were there like this—enormous and bulky, man-eating and unknown—lurking in the woods and rivers of America? How many people have been devoured over the years?

I saw something: a light ahead in the dark, on the same riverbank I followed. Slowly, I came to a stop, still low to the ground. I began to inch forward once more, now more aware than ever of how loud every movement was. Through the trees, behind a bush, I stopped and pushed myself up. My hand covered my mouth as I saw there the sheriff and captain of the fire department, with flashlights in hand, staring at the massive thing.

Now that it was in the light of those flashlights, I could see how the beast's eyes were blown out and ragged, pupils like irregular starbursts against the putrid yellow of its sclera. They bulged like tumors from its flesh, and thick scars crossed its thick hide. Silent, I suddenly realized that the two men were talking.

"Spit it out!" the sheriff demanded, as if talking to a dog. "Spit!" For a long moment, there was nothing.

"Do we have to get the chainsaw?" the captain asked, only for the sound of retching to fill the air. The throat of the creature bulged, and slowly, that great maw opened, tongue spilling from it. There, in the grasp of its tongue, was Jimmy's body, dead and gone. The sigh that came from the two men was audible, and the captain spoke up again. "Just throw him in the river, then?"

"Mmhmm," the sheriff grunted. "It won't take him again, and the morgue will just say he hit his head and drowned. Damn shame, too, he was a nice kid. Wonder what got the ol' bastard all riled up?"

"Lack of food, maybe."

There was a pause, a grunt, and then a splash, as I knew that Jimmy's body had just been shoved off into the water again. Then an even larger splash, as the creature went back into the water, submerging itself back into the river and vanishing from view.

I stayed there behind the boulder for what seemed like hours, even though I saw my watch count only 20 minutes. After the two men left, I waited another 20 minutes and went back home. There was nothing I could say, nothing I could do. Apparently, the police and fire departments knew about the thing in the river. Apparently, sometimes it would just… devour someone, and they'd have to tell it to spit out the one it ate, like a mischievous dog. There wasn't even any horror in their voice, just the dull drudgery of routine.

In the morning, I told my brother I loved him, I believed him, and to never go down to the river again.

16
SWANSEA'S TOLL

I am, I believe, the last person to have seen George Swansea alive. I was certainly the last one who spoke to him, for he left my apartment shortly before one o'clock in the morning and his corpse was discovered at dawn.

The respectable papers said he had been torn apart by a beast of some sort that had wandered into the outskirts of the city. The cheaper ones made a fuss about the Ripper once more walking the streets of England. Neither included photos, and I am glad they did not—for I have no doubt now that what Swansea told me was true, and that his death must have been beyond imagining.

George Swansea and I did not know each other particularly well. We were acquaintances at the most, familiar with each other through a mutual friend. The truth was, we did not have much in common. I was—or rather, am still—an artist, sustained alternately on commissions from the *nouveau riche* and my own family's funds, while Swansea himself was a historian who specialized in ancient economics—certainly, an interesting subject. I understand he was well respected in his field, but he was only interested in art insofar as it was something the patricians of Rome would pay substantial sums for, and thus injected *denarii* into the economy.

Thus, it came as no small surprise when he knocked at my door at nine o'clock at night, just as I was retiring to bed. When I opened the door to begin complaining at whoever had thought it was a good idea to barge in so late, I saw him outside my apartment—a place I had no idea he even knew the address to.

Swansea was not a small man; he stood a good head and a half taller than me and weighed a dozen kilograms more, dressed in a suit that stood just on the edge of being ill-fitting. Sweat beaded on his forehead and shone in the lights of the lamps outside. As I opened the door, he mopped his forehead with a handkerchief in one hand, his other occupied with a briefcase.

"Swansea?" I asked, unsure of what I saw.

"Yes, it's me, Martin," he huffed. "Let me in, will you? It's cold as the devil out here."

"He lives in Hell, doesn't he?" I responded, but opened the door wide for him anyway.

The large man stepped in and closed the door behind him, stamping snow from his boots onto the ground. "Artistic man like you has surely read Dante's Inferno, haven't you?"

I conceded the point with a shrug and stepped back. "Take a seat. Would you like some tea?"

"No thank you," he answered me, taking a seat on the couch and mopping his forehead once again. "I don't expect to be here particularly long."

I took my own seat opposite Swansea. "Why are you here? Forgive my… bluntness, but if you were in trouble, I rather doubt I'd be the one you come to first."

"I take no offense," Swansea acknowledged, placing his handkerchief back in his suit pocket. "It's true. I don't believe I'm in trouble—I believe trouble has already found me and taken me for its own."

I blinked and leaned back. "And what in God's name do you mean by that, Swansea? Are you in debt, or something? Surely, if that's the case—"

The bark of laughter that came from the older man was like a gunshot. It echoed loudly through my apartment, as if it had been torn from him unwillingly, and there was an unspeakable bitterness to it.

"In debt! God, I suppose I am, though my creditor takes no collateral and no money. I came to you for two reasons, Martin. Firstly, that you are an artistically inclined and talented man, and while I may not personally see the merit, I am not so churlish as to entirely dismiss your abilities—and I wanted to ask your opinion on something.

"Secondly, it is exactly because we are mere acquaintances. Paradoxically, I fear your judgment on my foolish actions less than I would the scorn of a bosom friend. For I think I have been a fool enough to warrant... well, never mind that now. Here." He reached into the briefcase he had placed at his side and took out a ball of cloth roughly the size of my fist. Placing it on the table, he began to unwrap it and looked at me sternly. "Do not touch it, for the love of God, Martin. Believe I ask because it is old, or because it is cursed, or because it is fragile—whatever puts your mind at rest—but I beg of you: do not touch it."

I was stunned. Swansea had always seemed the scientifically minded type, not one for superstition. "Alright," I relented, "but surely you understand just how strange this is, Swansea!"

"I do," he said grimly. With that, he unfolded the ball of cloth the rest of the way, and it opened like a flower onto the table. In the center was a single coin. Small and unassuming, it was barely larger than a sovereign, silver-bright and gleaming in the lamp light. Shifting forward in my seat, I brought my face closer.

It wasn't mine. The thought blasted through my head like a thunderbolt, and I jerked backward. I knew it wasn't mine, obviously, so why had I thought that, and with such force, such overwhelming dread and a true, desperate fear of touching it with my own flesh? There was a part of me that wanted to touch it, now; the rational part of me howled at me for even considering it. It was just a coin, a circle of a metal alloy. Yet, just as I knew it was not mine, I knew something awful would happen if I touched it.

"You felt it too, didn't you?" There was no question in Swansea's voice as he spoke, even as he reached out and brushed his fingers across the surface of the coin in an action I nearly reached out to prevent. "The sense that it is not yours, will never be yours—and then that reaction, to prove yourself wrong. I did not listen to my own instincts, and thus... Well, I am dead already, I fear, and nothing on this earth can prevent it."

I shook my head, holding my pulsing skull in my hands. "You think it... what, cursed? Have you any idea how mad you sound?"

"Then explain what just happened," he spoke, annoyance in his voice. "I will not deny the evidence of my own eyes, even if it appears to be impossible, or magic, or a miracle or a curse. Explain it to me, Martin, and I will walk out of this room immediately."

For a moment, I struggled for words before I sighed. "Fine," I breathed, letting the air rush out of my lungs, refilling them once more. "You want my opinion on this coin?"

"Indeed," he answered, and tapped it with his fingernail, the sound ringing clear and making me shiver. "Take a look at the obverse, and tell me what you think."

"Fine," I repeated myself, and leaned over it once more. The obverse of the coin is what most laymen know as the "heads" side or the "face" of the coin. It typically displays the head in profile of a prominent figure. Indeed, that was what I expected as I focused on the gleaming metal, but instead, there was what looked like a scene of murder.

I had seen old coins before, some dating back to the Roman Republic. They were things that might once have been beautiful, but nevertheless rough and somewhat crude. For while with stone and marble the Romans stood with the Greeks in their sculpture and architecture, the truth was those ancient peoples did not have the ability to work metal as finely as we now did in the throes of the industrial era. And yet, I sincerely doubted even the most talented metalworkers would be able to create so fine and detailed a scene as on the obverse of this coin.

It depicted a man in a Roman toga staggering backward against a column, in the moment after a second man had wounded him with a blade. The blow seemed to be mortal, for it cut through from his left hip upward to his right clavicle, and blood was spilling down his torso and beginning to pool on the ground. His hand left a bloodstain on the pillar, and was further marking it with a bloody smear as the victim slowly fell to the ground, an expression of grief and pain on his face.

The second man was similarly dressed, if younger and unshaven, eyes alight with anger and face twisted in rage. He was frozen upon the coin still in the middle of his swing, muscles tensing and flexing in a way that even the most talented painter would be jealous of. Blood ran red upon the edge of his blade, and droplets of lifeblood drawn from his victim hung in the air.

There were no other people in frame, but there was a city. Perfectly marked buildings stretched to the very edge of the coin and abruptly cut off, as if there had been a great engraving on a single sheet of metal and a circle had merely been punched out of it. Simple buildings and great manors alike were on the coin, and I gasped as I saw the Temple of Jupiter Optimus Maximum in the background — tiny, barely the size of half a fingernail, yet clearly visible.

"What..." I whispered, my mouth suddenly dry and my throat swollen. Gulping, I leaned back and looked at Swansea, who returned my gaze evenly. "That is not possible," I told him, and shook my head as he began to frown. "I understand it lies in front of me," I forestalled, "and yet... I refuse to believe this coin was created longer than a decade ago. The skill and the machinery needed to create such a work of art on so small a scale… it did not exist before then. And if you purport that this is an ancient coin… No, it is simply impossible."

A humorless grin came across Swansea's face. "Ah, if only," he mused. "Yet I found it in a leather pouch, underneath a paving slab in an outlying Roman Empire era village—one the university has only recently been given permission to enter and excavate. This coin possibly comes from before the birth of Jesus. It does not come from after Nero's time."

I shook my head. "What in God's name…"

"That is not all," he said, and turned over the coin, showing me the reverse. I gasped. On it were the most lurid and explicit acts I had ever seen depicted, and some I frankly could not have imagined given a barrel of spirits and a dozen women of the night. Men and women alike coupled wildly on that side of the coin, with the same sex and opposite, wine pouring liberally from bottles and food rolling from cornucopias, their faces depicted in just as much pleasure as the two men from the obverse displayed rage and pain.

"Good Lord, man, turn it over again!" I cried, my face burning. The other man obliged, showing the murder once more. Huffing, I leaned back in my chair, focusing my gaze on the silver circle of impossibility. "Scenes of passion?" I remarked after a long moment. "Murder and anger on the obverse, pleasure and debauchery on the reverse?"

"My thoughts exactly," Swansea said, tapping it once more, letting the sound ring out like that of a bell, and continued to do so, forming a counterpoint to the ticking of the clock in the corner of the room, which did not so much interrupt my thoughts as form a beat for them to follow along.

"And yet... what could this have been used for?" I asked, leaning my head back and resting it against the plush cushion. "Surely these could not have been produced at any rate to allow use as currency—it must be commemorative, or something along those lines... And yet if that should be the case, why would they be under a paving stone in a yard?"

Swansea hummed for a moment, then we were silent. He sighed and shook his head. "It comes to mind," he murmured, "that I once spoke to a gentleman from America. He said he was an entrepreneur, and a collector of currency, though he professed himself as an amateur when it came to economics in general. We had a good conversation, and despite his claimed inexperience, there was one belief he held very strongly to."

"And what was that?" I asked, sitting up.

"That 'godly services must be paid for with godly coin,'" Swansea quoted. "That a layman or ordinary citizen may drop gold or silver—or the food he has farmed himself, should he lack all else—into the donation boxes of the temples, but the priests and occultists of the time who wished to make communion with their forces needed... a different currency."

For a long moment we paused, staring at that impossible coin, and a thought passed through my mind: would I go so far as to call this artwork divine? Miraculous? Godly? And therefore, would it not be possible for a divine coin, unlike an ordinary one, to know its owner and warn all others off? Suddenly, that bright and silver coin looked less like a circle of metal, and more like the glint of a blade—shining teeth in the dark.

"I think," said Swansea suddenly, "I should leave."

I turned to him, brow furrowed. "Swansea, are you..." He was on his feet before I could say anything else, and I noticed the sweat had beaded once more on his brow, his face clammy and pale.

"I can feel it," he murmured, as he frantically wrapped the coin back up in the cloth. "Like a tidal wave within me, surging and pulsing... passion and fury and lust and rage and desire, all echoing in my mind and body..."

I stood, slowly, from my chair, hoping not to draw his attention. Whatever had suddenly come over him, I had no guarantees it would not drive him to attack me. But he seemingly had no interest in me at all, merely grabbing his briefcase in one hand and that bundle of cloth in the other, before striding to the door and opening it.

In the frame of the door, he paused for a moment, before looking back at me. "I am," he pronounced solemnly, "off to throw the coin in the Thames, and hope none shall pick up this coin again. Goodbye, Martin." He slammed the door behind him, and I never saw George Swansea alive again.

I attended his funeral out of respect, though some of our mutual acquaintances expressed shock that we were that close. We weren't, I told them, but his death was shocking enough that I thought I should attend. Just to ensure a silver coin did not appear in his hand.

17
FINE PRINT

When I went to see the witch, it was half out of desperation and half out of spite for my grandma. She's a sweet lady, very religious, and has always been absolute pain in my ass. Doesn't matter if I hadn't fallen in with the cartel—they would have bled us dry with shakedowns within the year—and doesn't matter that I could buy her all the shit she'd ever want. She'd just looked at me and shake her head, pull me into an embrace, and kiss my forehead with tears in her eyes.

"You need to leave them, Luis," she told me constantly, "before you commit sins that God must ensure you are punished for." Grandma still thought I was a drug mule, then. I wonder what she would have thought if she knew the reason I got paid so much was because I was the guy they called in when they wanted someone to regret ever having been born. The thing about torture is, you don't do it for interrogation because they'll tell you anything to get the pain to stop. You do it to make an example.

Point is, I went to see the witch because the tides were turning inside the cartel. My boss was a man named Diego; I hated the bastard along with everyone else. He was cruel and sadistic, but he paid well to have me do my thing. Paid extra so he could watch, too. So, for me, Diego getting taken out was the worst thing that could happen. I was his man, and no one was going to want the psycho's pet psycho around. That meant when Diego got shot, I knew I was in big trouble. It wasn't just a matter of cash anymore; it was a matter of my life. I was in deep with Diego.

So, I went to the witch. Gloria was her name, and she didn't live on the outskirts of town or anything like some movie. No, she lived in a normal house on a normal street, but everyone just avoided it like the plague. No kids played there but a few who had the balls to throw a rock at the window, call her a witch, then scamper off to be praised by their friends. Had there ever been some reason why they started to call her a witch? I had no idea. All I knew was that my grandma called her a witch, and told me and my cousins to never, ever go near her. And if she ever talked to us, to not listen to a word she said. At the time, I had just come off a pretty damn big argument with her. I was all stressed out from Diego being in the hospital and she was still complaining about me being in the cartel. As I was walking back from the house I had bought her, I saw that goddamn street and figured *fuck it, might as well.*

I walked down her street, ignoring the tingle up my spine. I walked up her steps as a group of kids nearly broke their necks whipping their heads around to stare at me, and I knocked on the witch's door. There was silence for a few seconds, interrupted only by birdsong, until I heard wood on wood, and the door creaked open. I don't know really what I expected her to look like, but she looked like a grandma. She was short and wrinkled, a cane in one hand, wore a flowery dress, and looked up at me with dour eyes.

"What does the cartel want?" she asked, her voice flat and emotionless.

"Cartel wants nothing," I answered, shrugging. I'm a big man, but something in the way she looked at me gave me the creeps. At the time, I figured that it was just my superstitious grandma bouncing around the inside of my skull. I wasn't feeling too generous toward her then, so I ignored it. "I figured, hey, you're a witch, and I could use some help right about now, right?"

She looked at me, narrowing her dark eyes. "You're Luis, right?" Gloria eventually asked. "Alma's boy?"

"Yeah," I answered, nodding.

"Come on in then," she muttered, taking a step back. "Take a seat on the couch and don't touch any of my plants or books."

It took me a moment to choke back the urge to tell her I wasn't going to, but I had been raised to be polite to the elderly. So, I just nodded, went inside, and sat down. There was nothing special about the inside of her house; there were some paintings on the wall, some knickknacks here and there—looked kind of like the inside of an antique shop. She shuffled in from the other room, mug of something steaming in her hand, and took a seat on the chair opposite me. Taking a sip from it, she sighed and let her eyes flutter closed, before opening them again and staring at me.

"So, what do you want? Help, you said? I don't think someone like you needs help from an old woman like me." There was half a second where I thought about leaving, just getting up and heading out. But hey, I had already gotten this far, so I *might as well*, right?

I told her about how I was Diego's man, through and through, because even though I didn't like the sadistic nutjob, he paid incredibly well. And now that his enemies in the cartel were angling to take him out, I knew I was going to go with him when he eventually bit it, so I needed *something*. I had no idea what that something was, but I knew I needed it to stay alive—to keep making money, to keep doing my job. To keep doing my job, yeah, because even though I insulted Diego, *I* was the one who kept taking his money to impart violence on people who didn't deserve it. There was no way someone could keep on torturing and hurting men who begged for mercy, who begged to stop— who begged, eventually, for death—and not be affected by it sooner or later. But there I was, just trucking along without a care in the world. Truth was, I liked it as much as Diego, I just didn't show it. I had probably killed a couple hundred by now and tortured about half as many to death. That pain that I had inflicted was staining me like oil, infusing my flesh like some kind of fucked up marinade.

I blinked, and suddenly I realized my throat was sore from talking. It was pitch black outside, owls hooting and insects chirping. How long had I been here? How long had I been talking? What had I said? I shot up from my seat on the couch and fumbled for the gun at my side. I yanked it from my belt and pointed it at the woman in front of me.

"What the fuck did you just..." I trailed off and looked at the object in my hand. It was made of black metal, several inches in length, and had a grip I was holding onto. Slowly, I turned it, trying to think of what it could possibly be. Some kind of kitchen thing, maybe, but then why would I be holding it in Gloria's living room? There was a hole in the front of it, but I couldn't see anything down it, and there were a few switches on the side that I reached up to fiddle with.

"So," she said, interrupting my train of thought as my gaze flicked back to her and my hand dropped. "You want some way to keep your boss on top? Just keep him alive, huh?"

"Something like that," I agreed, dropping myself back on the couch and placing that weird object into my pocket. "As long as he's alive and keeps paying me, I couldn't care less."

Slowly, the old lady nodded, humming in her throat. "I can do that. But I'm not running a charity, you understand?"

Shrugging, I reached into my other pocket and pulled out my wallet. "Alright," I said, flipping through the stacks of cash I kept on me. "How much—"

"Oh, I don't need money, Luis," Gloria chuckled, taking another sip of her drink. "There are only two things I need you to do. First, your grandmother hasn't paid me yet. I did something for her, you know? Helped her get with your grandfather. Real fairy tale story, those two, but your grandma wasn't too keen on her end of the deal. So, you're gonna promise me what your grandma owes me."

I nodded. "Sure. And the other?"

"I want your darkness. You can think of that as a metaphor or as literally as you want, but I want your darkness. You understand me?"

"The hell does that mean?" I scoffed. "I'm not agreeing to anything vague like that."

"It's not vague," the witch spat, and she narrowed her eyes at me. There was a flash of nerves, but I scowled right back at her. "I want what makes you able to do violence like you do."

I leaned back on the couch and exhaled. "Then just say you want me to off someone for you, old lady. Fine, whatever, I agree."

"You sure? Don't want to find out you're like your grandma, going back on her debts."

"I said I agree," I growled at her, and stood up. "What are you gonna do about Diego?"

"I'll figure something out," she said, leaning back in her seat and taking another sip from her mug. "I've made the deal with you, and I keep my deals. Get out. It's late, and I'm tired."

"...Fine," I said, and I left.

When I went into Gloria's house, it was before noon. When I walked out, it was pitch black, and the moon was hanging low in the sky. I guess I had been in there talking for longer than I thought, but we had barely been talking for a few minutes, right? I had told her about my problem, and then…

With every step I took away from the house, I remembered more of how I just kept talking, about everything I spilled to her and how she just sat there, staring at me as I spoke of anything and everything that crossed my mind.

I swore, then, and reached into my pocket for my gun. I checked that the safety was still on with trembling fingers, that moment playing through my head on repeat—a flash of knowing what was in my hand, and then not. Of knowing it was a gun, a firearm, a pistol, a machine used by humanity for decades to kill people… and then suddenly not knowing anything about it.

That was what made me decide two things. One, that Gloria *was* a witch. It's one thing to know something in your head, though, and another to know it in your heart. Now this was both. The other thing: I wasn't going to go back and do anything about it. If she wanted my "darkness," whatever that meant, she could damn well have it. I would pay her, Diego would be safe, and I would keep breathing too.

And it worked out well, for a while. Diego got better. None of his rivals in the cartel or any government agencies took a crack at him. I took out some two-bit thug that had been pissing him off to cheer him up and went back home happy as ever. Stopped by to see my grandma, who was still upset about me working for the cartel. For a minute, I was tempted to tell her all about Gloria. I wanted to ask her about what on earth the witch was talking about with the whole payment thing, but I was mad at her, not ready for her to have a damn heart attack. Instead, for a couple of weeks, I just lived life normally.

I went back to her house after Diego had healed up. I knocked on the door once, twice, three times… and then I woke up on a bed, in nothing but boxers. I wanted to move, but I couldn't. My fingers didn't even twitch. I looked at them, desperately begging them to do anything at all. All I could do was stare up at the ceiling, even as I heard the clack of cane on wooden floor from somewhere out of sight.

"I love it when complicated problems have simple solutions," Gloria's voice came from somewhere. As the sound of a lighter went off, the smell of smoke wafted through the air. "Know what your grandma promised me in exchange for making your grandfather fall in love with her? It's a classic one, really: firstborn child! Of course, I was still quite young back then and didn't word that bargain quite as tightly as I should have. So here we are, sixty years later, and still no payment for my services. Insulting, really. Until you came along."

A finger, cool and wrinkled, stroked my cheek, patting it before withdrawing. I felt a cold wetness on the inside of my elbow, right where the vein was. That was the moment I really started to lose it. At least, I wanted to. But I couldn't. My mind was racing, and I wanted to struggle against whatever was keeping me paralyzed and limp. But my heart refused to beat quicker, the expected adrenaline absent from my system. I was in the worst danger I had ever been in, and I couldn't move at all.

"I've been needing some darkness—and I don't mean that metaphorically, sorry to tell you. I mean it literally. But getting some darkness isn't as easy as walking down the street and borrowing a cup of flour from the neighbors. You, though, Luis… you're practically soaked in it. Sadism, cruelty, violence… but more than that, the banality of it. How you don't care in the slightest, because for you, it's nothing more than something that gets you paid. You can look down here, Luis."

I did, my eyes moving down to where a needle had been placed in my arm. I didn't feel it go in; I didn't feel it at all. As I watched, something began sliding up the clear tube, dropping bit by bit into the container at the end. It was black and thick and like tar. The idea of it inside my body made me want to vomit into my mouth worse than any bloody corpse I had ever produced.

"Good quality, too," Gloria hummed. The dual horror being used like livestock and being unable to even move made my vision blur.

Finally, I blinked and realized that wasn't why my vision was blurry. No, with each passing second the flesh was vanishing from my bones. Sucked up, liquefied, and mixed into that jet-black slurry filling that glass container.

"Sorry about all this... but you did promise me your darkness. Unfortunately, that's not something I can just rip out and leave the rest of you be. Your own fault for not paying attention to the details of our agreement, I suppose. It's a part of you, whether you like it or not... and it's all mine, now. Nice doing business with you."

18

LURE

When I was six, an old man taught me how to fish. I only remember him vaguely—in flashes of crooked teeth, leathery skin, and a creaking voice—but I remember his words.

"They can't see proper," he murmured, pointing with a bony finger at the clear water, where a trout as long as my young arm swirled around his hook, probing it before darting away. "Got no idea that the riverbank is up 'ere, do they? Gotta bait 'em proper, 'nd reachin' down inta the water won't work. So patience."

He was a friend of my grandfather, I think. I'm nearly as old as my grandfather was then, so perhaps it is expected those details have slipped my mind.

I have a doctorate in theoretical physics. I got it back when the economy wasn't in such bad shape, when you would still get paid an impressive salary sitting in an office doing math of theoretical importance. Discovering the underlying nature and equations of the universe is exciting to scientists and students, but less so for the accountants. It is a constant balancing act between prestige and finance, and as soon as the latter begins to outweigh the former, I was always the first to go. It did mean, however, that I had a curriculum vitae a mile long, and an equally long list of administrators eager to assure me there were no hard feelings on their part for cutting me loose. I couldn't say the same from my part, but they were useful contacts and eventually got me the job I have kept for nigh on two decades.

That day, I got a letter emblazoned with three words—Department of Defense. Perhaps to my colleagues in the humanities, this might have been cause for alarm, but the government has long been a patron of the physicists and engineers. Thankfully, that was the case with this letter:

We believe you would be an asset to the groundbreaking research that has been carried out continuously by this country...

A phone number was included, and so naturally I called to arrange an interview.

I met my interviewer at my home: a man who introduced himself as a Mr. James Evans. There was no military installation near the college town I lived in at the time, and a restaurant wasn't secure enough, so I was told. He was a short man, cleanly shaven and bald, with a slight smile on his face as he took a seat and spoke to me in my sitting room.

"I would be your supervisor, should you accept the position," he told me, briefcase on the coffee table in front of him. "As I'm sure you may understand, there really isn't much I can tell you, prior to your signing of the paperwork and NDAs. There are some... exceptionally strict legal penalties should you discuss the work with anyone not qualified."

"Prison?" I asked.

"For life," he confirmed. "Possible court-martial and summary execution, if you spoke of it to the Soviets or the Chinese." At that, I must have recoiled, because his smile widened. "The Department of Defense takes this project exceptionally seriously, Dr. Dubois, and I think it would be best to impress these penalties on you immediately—before you sign on."

I hesitated for a moment. If these penalties were so severe... it was possible what I was signing onto was a new Manhattan Project. Something that might leave my name in history as more than a curiosity for equally niche scholars. Perhaps a selfish wish, but one I think everyone has had at some point. A desire to make sure that you aren't swept away in the ever-moving tide of history. And so, before Evans left, I signed under his approving gaze. Within a month, my background check was cleared of communist influence and that of other unsavory individuals, and I was on a plane to Oregon.

Evans met me there, shaking my hand firmly and leading me out of the airport to the car, where a soldier in uniform waited. He took my luggage and loaded it as I stepped into the car alongside my new supervisor.

"Have you ever lived here before, Dr. Dubois?"

I started, flicking my gaze from the man closing the trunk and walking around to the driver's seat to Evans, who sat opposite me with that same mild smile.

"When I was young," I answered. "I moved away when I was eight or so."

"My son is around the same age," Evans said, "and he's turning out to be quite the intelligent young man! Teachers are beginning to be stumped with what to do with him."

"You must be proud," I murmured, to a nod from the man sitting opposite.

"Certainly!" he agreed, and for the rest of the ride I was regaled with tales of his son and the antics a young boy gets up to in rural Oregon.

The conversation was eventually cut short by the squealing of a metal chain-link gate slowly trundling aside. A uniformed man in the guardhouse looked at us, eyes darting over the driver, who was putting an ID away, and to us. He looked back down at his lap, and the truck moved on.

While the entrance to the compound was surprisingly lax, the interior of the building was not. It took an hour to get through the security station inside. Evans clapped my shoulder and assured me that "This is your first time here. It won't be as bad when you start working." We moved down the hallway and came to a stop at a steel door.

"Here it is," Evans said, pushing open the door. He started to say something else, but I couldn't hear him through the rushing of blood in my ears and sudden pounding of my heart. My eyes were locked onto it. I couldn't take them away, even as they began to water and wet my cheeks.

There is always, I think, a part of everyone that thinks they are normal, the world around them is normal, and that will always be the case. No, they say, *other* children see their parents get divorced, not mine. No, they say, *other* siblings don't come home from the movie theatre because of a drunk driver, not mine. No, they say, *other* wives are unfaithful and callous, not mine.

I thought I had long been past that stage. I thought I had accepted that life is ultimately random, and that this "normalcy" exists solely in the domain of television sitcoms. But when I saw that impossible object, the part of myself so enamored with "normalcy" I had thought no longer existed shattered for good.

There was nothing normal about that sphere, and therefore there could be nothing normal about someone seeing it. It hung in the air, exactly four feet off the floor. The ground below it was lighter than the rest of the room, despite the floodlights surrounding it, like a reverse shadow. The sphere itself was a forest green—no, a deep blue—no, a neon yellow. It changed colors with every moment, yet each time I was convinced it had always been that color, that my own memories were lying to me. Three deep wounds were etched into its surface. "Wound" is the only word to properly describe those gouges, for they leaked a sap-like substance so thick it beaded in droplets that hung fat and heavy on the edges of the cuts. Yet it was clearly metal, shiny and reflective, like a steel orb with the diameter of a tire.

As I watched, I saw motion from that reverse shadow and had to stop myself from gasping as a bubble, which I wanted to dismiss as a mere trick of lighting, rose into the air. It hung there, barely a centimeter off the ground, and I felt my knees buckle as I realized it was rising, slowly, up to the sphere.

"This object," Evans said, "appears to experience time in reverse."

A shiver ran up my spine, and I thought to shush him, even though he was speaking in a normal voice. There was something equally awe-inspiring and terrifying about that impossible object, something that demanded attention, causing mere conversational tone to ring like a gunshot in my ears.

"It has, over the past ten years since its discovery, regained approximately six percent of its total volume. As for the object's mass, we have no idea at all. As far as we have been able to tell, it is made of a single substance, but it corresponds to no known element or compound. We have attempted to introduce other substances into the sphere, and the reactions have massively varied. Your job will be to study this sphere, to understand how such a thing might operate, and to assist the other members of your team in figuring it out."

I stepped forward, and slowly walked around the sphere, Evans patiently waiting. The very beginning of a bubble was forming in the reverse shadow below, nothing more than the slightest curve coming up from the light on the floor. I reached out to touch it, before jerking back, and stepping away.

"Do we know if it is safe to touch?" I asked in a hushed whisper, to which Evans nodded.

"Yes. If you'd like to do so, you can."

I glanced back at him. "How did you discover that?"

His smile was thin. "Rats."

Gulping, I leaned forward and pressed my hand against the sphere. It was warm to the touch and felt like nothing more than the hood of a car that had been resting in the summer sun. For some reason, that was what sent me stepping hurriedly away from that impossible object, that it would feel so normal on my skin despite everything else about it. No, it shouldn't feel like that at all. Staring at it for a moment more, I was interrupted by a pat on my shoulder from Evans.

"Well, let's get you down to meet the rest of the folks studying it. Believe me, you'll see it so much you'll get sick of the damned thing!"

I met the rest of the scientists and engineers studying the thing I learned that had been nick-named *the hourglass*. There were nine people in total, and I was the tenth to arrive. The most experienced among them had worked on the hourglass for ten years, the least experienced for two, and collectively, they had no idea what to make of it. One group thought it could be alien in origin, as in the science-fiction movies of the day. Others held it was an entirely natural, if rare phenomenon. I was undecided at first. But now, for twenty-odd years, I have been employed by the Department of Defense to study the hourglass, and we have made no progress on it.

For years, we have written equation after equation, desperately struggling to come up with a model of physics in which such a thing might be possible, but we cannot seem to make it make any sense at all. It sits in the middle of the air, as if to mock us. The very act of its levitation is enough to spark a hundred papers and arguments about gravity—and that is the least of the impossible properties it possesses. The fact that it seems to exist in reverse, the act of its wounding being continuously undone consumes all those who newly arrive to work at this facility. And yet, as time passes, they all discover something new about it.

I, for instance, discovered that the equations I drew for the rate at which sap rises up to the hourglass fails the second derivative test. Such a thing cannot be possible in nature. There will always, without fail, be some variance in data that would cause the second derivative to vary wildly, and yet here it was a perfectly flat line.

The next individual to come to the project, Dr. Amelia Moore, realized that the hardening of the sap into the substance the sphere is made of shares certain similarities to that of actual sap, and so the hourglass is made of a type of amber, not some manufactured material.

At least, this is what we think. For twenty-odd years, I have worked for the Department of Defense on this impossible sphere, and for all those years, I have seen more and more scientists arrive to study it. At first, it was only one a year; last month, we welcomed six new members to the team. I feel, sometimes, like we are nothing more than birds pecking at a plastic cup, desperately trying to understand something so far out of our frame of reference that there is no hope of understanding it.

When I was six years old, an old man taught me how to fish. I remember him more with each night that passes, and constantly wake up in chills, my sheets soaked clean through with sweat. He wasn't my grandfather's friend. I know that for sure, now, because I remember my grandfather hurrying me away from that fisherman with nervous glances over his shoulder. I would say I am remembering those details that had faded away with childhood, but I am certain he did not appear in real life as he does in my dreams.

His teeth were crooked and yellow and seemed to almost overflow from his chapped, thin lips, and I swear he holds them in a bared grin longer and longer every night. Skin like leather practically hung off his bones like folds of fabric and swayed in the breeze that came down from the mountains. I do not think he ever opened his eyes, yet he looked right at me, and I saw his orbs twitch beneath his eyelids. Constantly, I find myself miscounting his overly long fingers in my memory, and I no longer think he had fingernails at all.

He was not human. He *is* not human, I should say. He still exists, though *still* may be the wrong word for a creature like him.

Time is a river, you see, and we swim within it, following the current for all our lives. We have no ability to conceive of the riverbank, where an old man who is not human sits with a fishing rod.

As the brightly colored bait jerks about in the waters of time, leaking sap and confounding those within, he smiles with those crooked teeth, waiting for a bite.

THANK YOU

Thank you so much for reading my book. I hope you enjoyed reading it at least as much as I enjoyed writing it.

If you've got a spare moment, would you mind writing a review? I'd love to hear which story was your favorite.

You can leave one where you purchased the book, or at my publisher's website below. Sincerely, THANK YOU!

https://hylosis.pub

ABOUT THE AUTHOR

https://hylosis.pub/pages/author-alphonse-schaller

Alphonse Schaller was born in Southern California and raised in a house with a bookshelf in every room. A regular visitor to libraries, he fell in love with the horror and dread of H.P. Lovecraft and Jorge Luis Borges, as well as the sweeping fantasies of Robert Jordan and Brandon Sanderson. He started writing in the third grade and has much improved since. Zone Rouge is his first collection of short stories. He is also known as Rowan Cullen.

ABOUT THE PUBLISHER

https://hylosis.pub/pages/publishing

Hylosis Publishing is an independent publisher located in Chandler, Arizona. We firmly believe everyone has a story to tell or a unique perspective to share. We are always on the lookout for talented thinkers and storytellers.

Interested in getting published? Apply using the link above.